Restless Breeze

A Nautical Novel

By
Ed Robinson

Copyright 2017 by Ed Robinson

Leap of Faith Publications

This is a work of fiction. Real people and real places are used fictitiously. Although some of the events described are loosely based on my true life experience, they are mostly products of my imagination.

For my father, who was always his own man.
I have always been proud to be his son.

"**The Schofield Kid:** It don't seem real. How he ain't gonna never breathe again, ever. How he's dead. And the other one too. All on account of pulling a trigger.

William Munny: It's a hell of a thing, killing a man. You take away all he's got and all he's ever gonna have.

The Schofield Kid: Yeah, well, I guess they had it coming.

William Munny: We all have it coming, kid."

(From *The Unforgiven,* starring Clint Eastwood)

"Beware that, when fighting monsters, you yourself do not become a monster…
For when you gaze long into the abyss, the abyss gazes also into you."

Friedrich Nietzsche

One

I was having trouble coming to terms with the death of Bobby Beard. Not so much that he was gone, but that I had killed him. Maybe if I'd have shot him, it would have been less personal, but that's not what happened. I'd beaten him to death with my bare fists. I wasn't proud of it, just the opposite. I was ashamed.

Ever since I'd dropped out of society and gone off the grid, I had survived using cold logic. I was proud of my constant situational awareness. I was proud of my ability to always keep my cool, even in the most dangerous situations. That all went by the wayside down in Guatemala. I'd lost control. I'd become a savage, if only for a few minutes.

It shook me to the core whenever I allowed myself to think about it. At first, I was able to ignore it. Brody and I were living a dream life. We'd hopped from island to island, soaking up the sun and sharing our new love. We stayed on the move, running from our old lives, constantly seeking new shores. I avoided any destination that might have brought up old memories. I didn't want anything to come between us. In order to skip a stop in Luperon, where an old lover of mine lived, we made a risky run straight into the trades from the Turks and Caicos to Samana in the Dominican Republic. We took a beating as a result. Brody handled it well. She didn't ask why we didn't take the easier path. I guess she figured I had a good reason.

We tried our best to live in the moment and not to discuss our past. Brody knew I'd been on the wrong side of the law more than once. I assumed she had some demons she hadn't revealed to me, but I didn't ask about them. We didn't dawdle in the British Virgin Islands. I'd spread my wife's ashes in the surf on Norman Island. Instead, we motored from the USVI to Anguilla and St. Martin. We curved our way south to St. Kitts and Nevis. We visited Antigua and Barbuda. We made stops in Guadeloupe, Dominica, Martinique, St. Lucia, Barbados, and Grenada.

We had no ultimate destination. We had no time schedule. We explored the islands, visited with the locals, and pulled up anchor whenever the mood struck and the weather was right. From Grenada, we cruised off the coast of Venezuela. We did not stop due to reported civil unrest. Socialism had finally run out of other people's money in Venezuela, apparently.

We found ourselves anchored near Bonaire after a year of travel. The equator acted as a crossroad. We were indecisive as to which way to go next, so we stayed for a few weeks. That's when I started seeing Bobby in my dreams. I saw his lifeless body behind a floating door. I saw myself beating the life out of him. Ultimately, there was no running from what I'd done. I tried to appease myself by remembering what happened afterward. Bobby used his last breath to tell his family that it was his own fault. The locals down there hadn't given me up to the police, even though they knew what happened. No one was looking for me. There was no warrant for my arrest. I might have been innocent of a crime in the eyes of the law, but in my heart, I was guilty. I'd taken another man's life. It was only vaguely a matter of self-defense. I could have stopped when the fight was won. That's the moment when I went off the rails. I should have stopped. Being the victor should have been enough. I'd been challenged. I'd won. I could have walked away with my head held high, a winner.

I can't explain the primal urge that came over me at that moment. That was part of the problem. There was no logical explanation for what I'd done. I lost touch with my humanity for a brief period in time. The results were disastrous. How could I know that it wouldn't happen again?

Brody knew something was up. I couldn't help disturbing her when I woke up from the dreams. I tried my best not to withdraw from her emotionally, but she could sense that something was wrong.

"You want to tell me about it?" she finally asked.

"Killing Bobby Beard," I said. "I'm having some trouble processing what happened."

"It's been over a year," she said. "The best year of my life, I might add. Why now?"

"Being with you has helped me keep it quashed," I said. "But I guess I couldn't keep it under wraps forever."

"Is it the dreams?" she asked.

"I'm starting to not want to go to sleep," I answered.

"I'm here to listen," she said. "You can tell me as much or as little as you like. That's how we've been handling this relationship. Just so you know, I've got some experience in this area. Maybe I can help."

"You're about to tell me something that I didn't know about yourself," I said. "You don't have to do that."

"It's time," she said. "We've been living a fantasy. It's been a wonderful, glorious year, but we have to return to reality at some point."

"Do we?" I asked.

"I think we need to work through your guilt," she said. "We've got to put it behind us if we want to continue our fantasy."

"It's not just the guilt," I said. "It's more than that."

"You're questioning your motives," she said. "You're wondering how you could allow yourself to kill."

"How would you know that?"

Brody bit her lower lip and walked out onto the back deck. She put her hands on her hips and stared out at the blue Caribbean Sea. The sunlight silhouetted her figure. It was a sight to behold. I went to her. She faced me and looked directly into my eyes.

"I killed a man," she admitted. "I shot him in cold blood. That's why I was on hiatus in the first place."

I pulled her to me and hugged her for a long time. We'd gotten quite close over the past year. I thought this was one weird way to get even closer. We were both killers, not in a blood-thirsty serial killer kind of way, but we'd each taken another man's life.

"Do you want to talk about it?" I asked.

"I think it might help you," she said. "Maybe it will help us both."

"Tell me what happened," I said.

"I was chasing a perp," she said. "My weapon was already drawn. He stopped, turned around, and reached into his jacket. I put a couple of holes in his chest."

"Was he armed?"

"No, he wasn't," she said. "But I did what I'd been trained to do."

"What did it feel like to pull the trigger?" I asked.

"I've got to tell you," she said. "I was pumped. Blap, blap, two rounds center mass."

"But?"

"The rush lasted about two seconds," she admitted. "Then we saw that he had no gun. It all went to hell after that."

"What did the Bureau do?"

"Typical stuff," she said. "I got some paid time off. They did their investigation and cleared me. To them, it was a righteous shooting. I wasn't so sure."

"Sounds righteous to me," I said.

"You weren't the one who pulled the trigger," she said. "Just like you, I struggle with the taking of someone's life."

"So much that you couldn't return to duty?"

"The Bureau counseled me, gave me some reading material," she said.

"Did it help?" I asked.

"Somewhat."

"What was the gist of the helpful stuff?"

"That I'd done what I'd been trained to do," she said. "It had been drilled into me until I was conditioned to react like it wasn't even a conscious decision."

"I'm not sure that's helpful in my situation," I said. "I've been through no such training or conditioning."

"Survival instinct?" she asked.

"Only partially," I said. "Beat or be beaten sure, but I took it too far."

"What's your remorse level?"

"That's part of what I'm struggling with," I said. "I'm more concerned about how I acted than I am about Bobby being dead. I lost it plain and simple. I was not in control of myself, at least not for a minute or so."

"You were pushed to the breaking point," she said. "It happens. Think of some cop who thrashes a thug with his night stick. Everyone screams police brutality, but what has that cop been through? Everyone has a breaking point."

"I expect more from myself," I said.

"Okay," she said. "Let's explore what led up to the incident. What other factors were in play?"

"Holly," I said.

"Who's Holly?" she asked. "The woman to blame?"

"I don't blame her," I said. "Holly was my sometimes lover and a good friend. Much too young for us to make anything last. I thought she and Bobby were having a thing. It hurt."

"So when Bobby challenged you, you made him pay," she said.

"Something like that."

"It's an age old story," she said. "Men and their pride."

"But it's not that simple," I countered. "I went over a line. I stepped out of myself. Even animals rarely fight to the death. The old bull whups his challenger and goes back to his harem. The young bull licks his wounds and lives to fight another day. That cop with the night stick didn't beat the thug to death. He took out the challenge to his authority, but stopped short of murder."

"The people in Guatemala didn't think it was murder," she offered.

"Expats and outcasts in a third world country," I said. "I guess that qualifies as a jury of my peers."

"So what do we do now?" she asked.

"I seemed to dwell on it less when we were moving," I said. "Where do you want to go?"

"Can I be honest with you?" she asked.

"Of course you can," I said. "Tell me anything."

She took a deep breath before grabbing two beers. She handed me one, opened hers, and began to speak.

"Don't get me wrong," she said. "This has been great. Better than great. I will do this forever if that's what you want to do."

"But?"

"I miss America," she admitted. "I miss a decent grocery store, hot running water, fast food, and even television. Please don't hate me."

"I could never hate you," I said. "I'll tell you a little secret. I miss some of that stuff too, except for TV."

"Can we go back to Florida?"

"We'll turn this old tub north in the morning," I said. "But be patient. It's a long way."

"That's a load off my mind," she said. "I was afraid to bring it up."

"We're a team, Brody," I said. "We're in this together."

"You remember that too, the next time Bobby's ghost comes calling," she said.

Two

I sat down with my chart book that night. The word Guatemala was printed in big, bold letters to our north. I'd sworn I would never return, but I was second-guessing myself. Should I go back and try to make things right? Would Big Mike at Texan Bay shoot me on sight? Would Holly even want to talk to me? Was there anything that I could do or say that would smooth things over with either of them?

I sat frozen with indecision until Brody came to my side.

"What's the plan, captain?" she asked.

"I'd like your input on something," I said.

"Shoot."

"Guatemala," I said. "The folks at the marina and Holly. Should I attempt to resolve things with either of them?"

"Will it help resolve your issues with killing Bobby?" she asked.

"It's not like I can tell him I'm sorry," I said. "But I can apologize to those that were involved."

"Do you still have feelings for Holly?" she asked.

"I think I've come to terms with that," I said. "It's for the best that we went our separate ways. Now I have you. Shit works out."

"Is she pretty?"

"In a surfer, hippie kind of way," I said. "She's a true free spirit. That's what I was attracted to."

"So you're asking me if we should go find your pretty ex-girlfriend so you can apologize?"

"Big Mike too," I added. "I'm asking for your opinion. Is it a good idea?"

"It might help you to move on," she said. "You need to get beyond this somehow."

"It isn't out of our way," I said. "Wouldn't hurt to try to find them."

"You don't even know where they are?"

"Holly left Rio Dulce along with Tommy," I told her. "They went to search for gold off the coast of Belize. Big Mike will still be at the marina. We can start there."

"Guatemala sounds exotic," she said. "Different from the islands we've been seeing."

"It's wild country," I said. "Third world except for the expat communities."

"Is it dangerous?"

"Petty theft mostly," I said. "We had a run-in with some local thugs, but we settled the matter."

"Sounds like a story waiting to be told," she said.

"I was trying to help Tommy when we got into a scuffle with some street kids," I began. "Bobby was with me. We had to rough them up a bit. They retaliated by raiding the marina."

"What did you do about it?"

"I recruited some of the liveaboards, found their hideout, and thrashed them," I said.

"Thrashed them?"

"Big Mike is an old brawler," I said. "He gave us the confidence we needed to go in and kick some ass. We whupped every one of them that didn't run away."

"You just don't seem like the violent type," she said. "You've shown no indication of it over the past year."

"I'd prefer that it was never necessary," I said. "But that's not the reality of it."

"So before the incident with Bobby, you kept your violent tendencies in check."

"I've had to defend myself or my friends from time to time," I said. "It's called being a man."

"You have an old-fashioned view of the sexes," she said.

"You mean the traditional view that's worked well for centuries?"

"I didn't call you a sexist," she said. "You're a man's man, but you appreciate women."

"I very much appreciate you," I said. "Hell, I love women. The world would really suck without them."

"Does it bother you that I'm not a feminine flower?"

"You're kidding right?"

"A little," she said. "But I'm an FBI agent, or at least I was. I can take care of myself."

"I have no doubt," I said. "I like that you're not a girly-girl. They don't last too long living on a boat."

"Past experience?"

"A story for another day," I said. "Now, do we go to Guatemala or skip it?"

"We go," she said. "Let's take care of business while we're in the area."

As soon as the weather was good, we made our way north. We entered the Rio Dulce River late in the afternoon. I chose to anchor in the big bay called El Golfete, rather than continuing to Texan Bay. Big Mike could wait until the morning.

"You look tense," Brody said.

"A little," I admitted. "I don't know what to expect."

"Let me loosen you up," she said, unbuttoning my shirt.

I started to unzip my shorts, but she stopped me. She turned me around and started massaging my shoulders. She pushed me towards the settee and told me to lie down. I did as I was told. I felt warm liquid being applied to my back. She rubbed me gently at first. It felt nice. Then her hands worked a little harder. She dug her knuckles in and kneaded my muscles like thick bread dough. She worked her way down to my lower back, really digging in. She continued to massage me for twenty minutes before easing up. The return to gentle rubbing was welcome. She nudged me over onto my back and started rubbing my chest. She lightly ran her fingers over my ribs and stomach. She took note of my arousal but didn't stop.

My zipper went down and my shorts went down. More warm oil was applied. She stroked me very gently. Her touch was like a feather. She was in no hurry. I relaxed and enjoyed the magic of her hands. Slowly, gently, she brought me to relief. It was a selfless and caring act. I never felt better. She was welcome to loosen me up anytime she cared to.

I pulled up my shorts and picked my shirt up off the floor. I realized that the oil she used was scented.

"I smell like a department store perfume counter," I said, laughing.

"It's lavender," she said. "And I like it."

"I'll need to shower," I said. "I can't go talk to Big Mike smelling like flowers."

"Can we get water at the marina?"

"Depends," I said. "He might run us off as soon as he sees us."

"Wait a while," she said. "I'll make us drinks and we'll watch the sunset. Just you and me in paradise."

She poured straight rum over ice and we took our drinks to the back deck. Storm clouds were brewing over the lush green hills. We looked at each other and smiled. A good rain would mean deck showers. We sipped our drinks and waited for the first drops to fall. I grabbed a bar of soap and we stripped down. We ran out on the bow and danced in the downpour. I soaped her up and she returned the favor. We turned in circles with our arms out to rinse off. The rain slowed just as we got rid of the soap suds. The sun returned and steam rose from the bay. We stood there naked as the sun slowly disappeared behind the hills.

When it blinked out, we applauded.

"Good night, sun," I said. "Please come back tomorrow."

A marauding horde of mosquitoes chased us off the bow and back inside. I went straight to bed. I slept like a man in a coma that night. I had no dreams starring Bobby Beard. It was a good, solid, deep sleep. I woke refreshed and ready to speak to Big Mike.

"What are we walking into here?" asked Brody.

"It's a marina that backs up to a jungle," I told her. It's in decent shape for this part of the world. Mostly Americans and Canadians. Big Mike is from Texas."

"What's your gut feeling?"

"I don't think he'll shoot me," I said. "I think he'll let me talk."

"What evidence or experience leads you to that conclusion?" she asked, sounding every bit the FBI agent.

"I've sat and drank beer with the man," I began. "I helped when it was needed. There were no real repercussions from what I did. He probably won't be pleased to see me, but he'll be curious as to why I'm here."

"You ready?"

"Let's do this," I said.

We lowered the dinghy and climbed aboard. Brody carried her handgun in a beach bag, just in case. We motored across the open water until we neared the marina. I hovered in the entrance, looking around. I thought I saw Big Mike in his usual spot. No one came out to greet us or wave us off. I tied off at the fuel dock and helped Brody up onto the pier.

As we turned to walk up the docks we saw Big Mike walking towards us. He had a Budweiser in one hand and an ax handle in the other. His expression was grim. We met there on the dock, face to face. He was bigger and tougher than me. I didn't want to fight him.

"You're the last son of a bitch I thought I'd see today," he said.

"I won't trouble you," I said. "Just came to apologize."

"And don't think I don't know who you are young lady," said Mike. "Your hair's longer and you're tanner, but I recognize you. You were down here poking around after Breeze left. Can't imagine what the two of you are doing together."

"Nice to see you again, Mr. Payne," Brody said.

"The name's Mike," he said. "Now what's this about an apology?"

"I'm truly sorry for the trouble I caused you, Mike," I said. "We were passing through and I wanted to put things right before we moved on. I doubt I'll ever pass this way again."

"I'm not sure an apology to me is appropriate," he said. "You'd do better tracking down Bobby's family. Apologize to them."

"That's something I hadn't considered," I admitted. "I doubt they'd talk to me."

"We don't have time for coddling and sympathy around here," he said. "You and me are square, as far as I'm concerned, but if it makes you feel better, apology accepted."

"Thanks, Mike," I said, extending my hand.

We shook hands. I looked him directly in the eye.

"I really am sorry for what happened," I said. "We'll get out of your hair now."

"It's a shame how things turned out," he said. "We could have used a man like you down here."

"You have any more trouble from those punks in town?" I asked.

"Not a peep out of them," he said. "It's been quiet as a morgue around here lately."

"Peace in paradise," I said. "I don't want to do anything to disturb that. We are out of here to look for Holly and Tommy."

"Last I heard, they spend most of their time off the coast of Belize in that rust bucket of Tommy's," he said. "Going in and out of Ambergris for supplies."

"Good information," I said. "Thanks again."

"A word of advice," Mike said. "You're a hard man. You're smart and capable, not like these drunks around here, but you are really going to want to steer clear of trouble up there."

"What kind of trouble?"

"Different breed up there," he said. "Different vibe. Their thugs ain't kids. They're grown damn hard ass men. Some of them are vicious. Averaging a murder a week in Belize City these days. Away from the resorts, it's a dark and dangerous place."

"I was just hoping to find Holly and apologize to her too," I said. "Not intending to stick around."

"You do just that," he said. "Don't get mixed up in any wild schemes."

"I'll keep an eye on him," said Brody. "He's in good hands."

"Mind my words," he said. "Do not get into trouble in Belize. It won't work out so well for you."

Brody and I went back to *Leap of Faith*. I grabbed us each a beer and we sat down in the salon.

"Well?" I asked. "How do you think it went?"

"I think it went well," she said. "Don't you?"

"As well as could be expected," I said. "He's not exactly a teddy bear."

"I think he respects you," she said. "Probably doesn't see too many men like you down here."

"I'm pretty sure that bridge is burnt," I said. "I can't see any reason to ever come back here."

"Put it behind us," she said.

"Onward to Belize," I said. "You sure you're okay with meeting Holly."

"Do I have any reason to worry?"

"None whatsoever," I said. "I'm one hundred percent committed to you."

"And I to you," she said. "You, me and *Miss Leap*."

Three

We came out of the Rio Dulce and turned left at Punta Gorda. Following the coast kept us in the lee of the hills and out of the wind. I had Brody take the wheel while I studied the chart plotter. I tried to remember where Tommy had been looking for gold. The reef system was a mix of humps and valleys, with a variety of types of coral. It had been a year since I'd helped him survey the area. I drew an imaginary circle on the screen with my finger.

"This area here," I said. "We should be able to spot him from a long way off if he's out there."

We continued to motor north, searching the horizon with binoculars. It was mid-afternoon when I spotted the rusty old shrimper. It was anchored between two coral uprisings in deep water. I adjusted course to come alongside her port side. As we drew closer, I looked for a dive flag. None was displayed. Both outriggers were in the upright position. No one was underwater. I throttled down and floated fifty yards off. Then I saw Holly jumping up and down and waving. I eased in a little closer. Tommy threw some fenders over the side and motioned me in. Holly held up a handheld VHF.

I switched my radio to channel 72, which I knew she preferred to use.

"Breeze!" she yelled.

"Holly!" I hollered back.

"I can't believe it's you," she said. "What the hell are you doing here?"

"Looking for you and Tommy," I said. "Just happened to be in the neighborhood."

"Come raft up to us," she instructed. "Probably too deep for you to anchor."

We were in sixty feet of water. I only had two hundred feet of chain. I couldn't put out enough rode to hold us in rough weather. Tommy had lined his port side with a combination of big fenders and old tires. The swells were small and the sky was clear. I eased *Leap of Faith* alongside and Brody tossed lines over to Tommy and Holly. Once we were securely tied up, Holly scrambled aboard and gave me a big hug.

"I figured that I'd never see you again," she said.

"Likewise," I said. "But circumstances change. This is Brody. Brody, this is Holly."

The two of them shook hands and exchanged pleasantries. Holly's dreads were longer and more knotted. She wore a wetsuit and probably hadn't showered in days. She still looked good. Tommy was sporting a five-day stubble.

"Could use your help," he said. "Thanks for dropping by."

"What have you gotten into now?" I asked.

"He's put us on a pile of gold," Holly said. "But we've got some issues."

"Let me stop you both right there," I said. "Brody and I have spent the last year lounging on Caribbean beaches and avoiding any hint of trouble. It's been real nice. I didn't come here to mine treasure. I came here to apologize."

"We've put all that behind us," said Holly. "We don't talk about it or even think about it."

"Well, I haven't," I said. "I'm trying to work through some issues. I thought apologizing to you two would help. So indulge me, please."

"Say your piece," Tommy said.

I looked at Holly. She shrugged and nodded.

"Go ahead," she said. "Then it's my turn."

"I know I scared you, Holly," I began. "I would never hurt you, I hope you know that, but I was out of my mind for a minute. I can't explain it fully, but I'm sorry if I hurt you, or let you down. I can't take back what happened, but I am deeply regretful."

She stared at the deck.

"And Tommy," I said. "I know you don't need any excitement surrounding your operation. You didn't need the trouble that I caused. I screwed up, and for that I'm sorry."

"We figured some kind of law would come snooping around sooner or later," he said. "So we left. No big deal really. No one caught onto my scent."

"It was my fault," said Holly. "I've done really well suppressing that fact, until just now. You showed up and I'm faced with it again."

"You're blameless in this," I said. "What are you talking about?"

"Bobby," she said. "You know."

"I alone am responsible for my actions," I said. "Doesn't matter what you did."

"And I'm responsible for mine," she said. "Okay, so I messed around with him. He talked about staying down here permanently. We were flirting with the idea of being together. Where'd that leave you? You came all the way from Florida to Guatemala because of me. Face it. It's my fault."

"As you can see," I said, looking at Brody. "I've moved on. I'll always carry a deep appreciation for our time together. You're a special woman. I'm sorry for how it ended. I don't hold you responsible in any way. You shouldn't either. I'm the one who screwed up, in more ways than one."

"Will you help us?" she asked. "We really need your help."

"You show up out of the blue and you're just the man for the job," said Tommy. "You're a gift from heaven."

"What do you need us to do?" asked Brody.

Tommy and Holly looked back and forth at me, Brody, and each other. We'd been a good team once, but Brody was a wild card. They didn't know if she was capable or if she could be trusted.

"I'm not agreeing to anything yet," I said. "But let me assure you that Brody can handle herself. She's an FBI agent, or was anyway. I trust her with my life."

"FBI?" asked Holly. "I can't possibly see how this happened."

"If you've got any cold beer, I'll tell you all about it," said Brody.

"Sure," said Holly. "Come on inside."

Tommy pulled me away from the cabin door and led me over to the rail.

"You sure you want to leave them alone to have a girl talk?" he asked.

"Not sure if I could do anything about it if I wanted to," I said. "They're both pretty independent women."

"Holly's really something," he said. "Never seen anyone work like her. Never complains. She was born for this. Tell me about your new girl."

"She was FBI like I said. They'd been looking for me and no one could find me. I was too far off the grid. No phone, no computer, no bank account. They quit looking, hoping that I'd turn up. Then I was cleared, but Brody came looking for me anyway. She found me."

"Impressive," he said.

"That's what I thought," I said. "We clicked right away. It was just a matter of resolving our different sides of the law situation. Somehow we managed. She's smart and fearless. Now tell me what's going on."

"We're sitting on a pile right now, Breeze," he said. "Several million bucks."

"So what's the holdup?"

"It's a multi-faceted problem of logistics," he said.

"Spare me the engineering lingo," I said. "You got trouble with the locals?"

"That's obstacle number one," he said. "Every time we bring that outrigger over the side, a small boat runs out here to observe. If we bring up the gold, we'll have to fight them for it."

"What's obstacle number two?"

"Getting rid of the stuff," he said. "Just like before."

"Do you have any leads?"

"I do," he said. "But if he's dealing in recovered treasure, he'll know who I am. I can't risk the exposure."

"So you need me to broker the deal," I said.

"Just like before."

"Let's put all of our heads together," I suggested. "Work these problems through."

"So you'll help?"

"Didn't say that," I said. "Depends on what kind of plan we can come up with."

We went inside to find the girls. They stopped talking when we entered but gave each other knowing looks. I guessed they'd had a nice conversation about me. At least they were getting along. Holly was a good sport, and Brody was quick to adjust to new situations. They both handled themselves admirably. I couldn't figure out why these two unique and desirable women were attracted to me, but I was grateful.

I asked Tommy about the legal status of his search and recovery mission. It was all about the bribes.

"Every link in the chain is corrupt," he said. "I've bought good will from everybody but the damn president himself. That includes the Mexican Navy."

"Christ, how much did that cost you?" I asked.

"A little goes a long way down here," he said. "All they have to do is look the other way."

"What about the local pirates?" I asked. "They can't be bought off?"

"These particular dudes know what we're up to," said Holly. "They smell the gold."

"How would they ever sell it?" asked Brody.

"They probably haven't thought that far ahead," answered Holly. "They come out here quick, I tell you that. Must be keeping an eye on us from shore."

"I take it they're armed?" I asked.

"One holds a rifle," she said. "The others show pistols. They just grin at us and float out there."

"Now that we've got extra hands," Tommy said. "We can outgun them if necessary."

"I hope you mean that we can show equal or greater force," I said. "Not actually use it."

"There's usually three of them," said Tommy. "If Holly goes down to bring up some gold, we'll still have three armed guards up here. I think that will be enough to deter them."

"Couldn't we work at night?" I asked. "They won't see the gear moving in the dark."

"We're talking over sixty feet down," said Holly. "Visibility is poor in the daylight. It's taxing work without having to worry about carrying extra lights."

"What do you think about setting up a false alarm?" I asked. "Put the outrigger down and drop the basket. Fly the dive flag. Throw the air hose over. When they come running, all four of us are pointing weapons at them."

"Might deter them from coming out again," Tommy said.

"Or not," said Holly.

"Do you mind if I make a suggestion?" asked Brody.

She hadn't had anything to say up until that point in the conversation. Everyone turned to her and paid attention.

"Why not sneak ashore and disable their boat?" she said. "They don't know Breeze and me. We can go case the marina and figure out how to shut them down. We come out and you two start hauling up the booty."

"It might work," said Tommy. "If you two are willing to give it a shot."

"I took a picture of them with my phone," said Holly. "Cell service sucks but at least it still works as a camera."

"Holly's boat is at the Belize Yacht Club Marina," said Tommy. "These clowns are coming out of a private dock a little up the beach, by a place called Ramon's."

"It's worth taking a look," I said. "Brody and I can get a slip and take a casual stroll. Scope it out."

"The sooner the better," said Tommy. "We've been sitting on top of this pile for too long now."

"We'll head in tomorrow," I said. "Be prepared to start diving at any time."

We all took bathroom breaks and got new beers. We'd found a potential solution to our first problem, thanks to Brody. I was proud of her contribution and told her so.

"I just have one reservation," she said.

"What's that?"

"Big Mike's admonishment," she said. "Don't get into trouble in Belize, remember?"

"I don't sense trouble yet," I told her. "I might tomorrow, but it's more likely to come when we try to sell the stuff."

"Then we need a plan for that," she said. "I reserve the right to back out at any time."

"I haven't fully committed us yet," I said.

"Sure seems like it," she countered.

"We'll both sleep on it," I said.

It was then that we all noticed increased motion of the boat. I stepped outside to take a look at the seas. The wind had picked up and dark clouds were spinning up over the coast.

"You got weather radar on this tub?" I asked Tommy.

"The old fashioned kind," he said. "Good for twenty-five miles, if you know how to read it."

"Tell me which way the storm is headed," I said.

Tommy bent over the green glowing screen and watched for a minute or two. Holly peered over his shoulder.

"It's almost stationary," he said. "Maybe even inching inland."

"Okay, thanks," I said.

Brody was checking the lines that held us alongside the shrimper. I didn't like the way they were rubbing. If it got worse, one of them would give way. The steel hull of Tommy's shrimper would bust up *Miss Leap* in short order. I was faced with a dilemma. It was too late to make it into the marina, plus that's where the storm was at its worst. I wasn't ready to enter a strange place, in the dark, in rough seas. That was stupid. I couldn't stay tied to Tommy either. There was no way I could reasonably get a good anchor set in the deep water. The shallow water was also closer to the storm.

A big wave picked my boat up and banged her into the shrimper. The wind was picking up.

"We've got to cut loose," I yelled.

"Where are we going to go?" asked Brody.

"We'll have to ride it out," I said. "Get ready to take the lines in."

Holly and Tommy stood at the ready while I started the engine. I timed the waves so I wouldn't take a big one just as we got free. I yelled "now" as I pushed the throttle forward. I could hear everyone else yelling down below.

"You're free," said Holly.

"Shove off, captain," said Tommy.

"I've got the lines," said Brody. "Go."

I was already going. I kept the bow into the waves and surged away from Tommy's boat. Brody joined me on the bridge. We were banging pretty hard until we got a few hundred yards away from Tommy's boat. I eased back on the throttle until we were barely making way.

The bow would rise up as the waves rolled under us. Then we'd surf down the backside as the stern rose up. The blocky waves were close together, giving us no rest. Something clattered in the salon below. We hadn't had time to secure things for a rough ride. I had no weather radar, so I couldn't keep tabs on the storm's progress. Tommy had said it might be inching inland. I had a decision to make. I could simply hold our position and hope the waves abated soon, or turn and run away from the storm. I chose to run out to sea, away from the wind field of the storm. First I'd have to get *Leap of Faith* turned sideways to the waves, which she hated. I didn't much care for it either. When we turned, there was a brief moment of panic as we heeled hard to port. I goosed the throttle for all it was worth and spun the wheel until the waves were on our stern. *Miss Leap* righted herself and wallowed along in the mean following sea. It was no place for anyone prone to seasickness, but Brody and I managed to keep our beers down.

"Holly shit, Breeze," said Brody. "That was a risky move."

"You all right?" I asked.

"I'm fine except for peeing my pants a little," she said. "What possessed you to turn like that?"

"Sorry, I should have warned you," I said. "Snap decision. I've had her over on her side like that once before. She popped back up. I thought it was worth the risk."

"Here's to heavy old boats with a full keel," she said. "Good job *Miss Leap*."

We rolled and bucked along a course that led us away from shore and the storm. The seas gradually lessened. We were twenty miles out in the ocean before it was calm enough to assess the damage. Nothing was broken in the salon. Some cabinets had opened and spilled non-breakables onto the floor. We straightened up, let our heart rates return to normal, and caught our breath. The storm appeared to be moving inland as Tommy suggested. The danger had passed.

"What now?" Brody asked.

"We just idle around out here until dawn," I said. "I'll take first watch. Go get some rest."

Brody went below to lie down. I climbed back up to the bridge. Off to the east, the sky was clear. I kept my speed low, puttering along at three knots, first north and then south. I thought about the situation we now found ourselves in. Just like that, we were knee deep in intrigue and danger. I'd had a year's reprieve from missions like this one. I really enjoyed the time off, but now I could feel my blood pumping. I didn't ask for it, but there it was. I only wanted to make things right with Holly. She and Tommy had sucked me in too easily. They knew that I couldn't say no.

This time I had Brody. I had to consider her safety and her feelings about the matter. Did she really want to participate in whatever scheme was about to go down? If she wasn't willing, I'd have to disappoint Tommy and Holly. Brody had to come first. Hell, I'd be disappointed if she wanted out, but I was determined to make this relationship work. So far we'd had no problems at all. This would be our first real test as a couple. Up until then, we'd floated along through heaven on Earth.

I let Brody sleep for three hours before waking her. We were at a dead idle, just floating in two hundred feet of water. There was no sign of the earlier storm or any other disturbance. She'd have an easy shift.

"Morning Glory," I said. "Just slowly angle us towards shore. We'll hail that marina after the sun comes up."

"Sweet dreams," she said. "Three hours?"

"It will be close to daylight by then," I said. "Yell at any sign of trouble."

The excitement of the day had worn me out. I dropped off into a deep sleep immediately. I found Bobby there. He was in a hospital bed with an oxygen mask on and assorted tubes connected to his body. I saw the heart monitor blinking. I watched until I could no longer see him. All I saw was the monitor. It stopped blipping up and down. There was nothing but a flat line. Bobby was gone for the hundredth time.

I wanted to wake up, but it didn't happen. I saw Big Mike sticking a fat finger in my face. He was telling me to stay out of trouble in Belize. Brody joined him. They spoke in unison.

"Stay out of trouble, Breeze."

Brody ended my dreams with a gentle nudge.

"It's five in the morning," she said. "Not light yet. You want more time?"

"No," I said. "No. I'm good."

"Coffee's on," she said. "It will be ready in a minute."

I splashed some water on my face and looked in the mirror. Some middle-aged dude looked back at me. He had a smattering of gray in his hair and beard stubble. The sun had burned deep into his skin. His eyes were blue and bright. My youth was long gone. With it had gone my previous life. I was a boat bum now, finding my way in a world that felt alien to me. I still hadn't succumbed to cell phones and computers. The only possessions I cared about were my boat and whatever tools it took to fix and maintain her. I had the means and the partner to stay away from reality forever. I'd achieved my dreams. So why was I so pumped about this mission? I needed to talk it over with Brody, but first, I needed coffee.

Brody handed me a cup as soon as I came up from below.

"Rise and shine," she said. "Did you get any sleep?"

"Doesn't feel like it," I admitted.

"The dreams?"

"Yup."

"We've got to do something about that," she said.

"I thought coming here was the first step," I said. "I make things right with Holly and Tommy and start to feel better about things."

"So we keep taking steps until the dreams stop," she said.

"About that," I said. "This whole idea of throwing in with them to help with the gold.

Are you certain you want to be a part of that? You don't owe either of them a thing."

"This is what you do, right?" she said. "I'm with you, all the way. I've been restless, Breeze. So have you. I can see it in your eyes. Let's have an adventure."

"If things go right, there won't be many adventures," I said. "But they seldom go right. Be prepared for the unexpected. Stay on your toes."

"He says to the G-man," she said. "I've got more training than you do mister."

"I reckon I have more experience in this type of operation," I said. "None are the same. You have to be ready to improvise in a split second. Trust your instincts."

"Will we be carrying weapons today?" she asked.

"Not until we get back to Tommy's boat," I said. "We're tourists this morning."

"Let's do this," she said.

Four

We tied up at the marina's fuel dock. I filled the tanks while Brody flirted with the dockhand. She asked harmless questions that gave her information. Where could we walk on the beach? Can we snorkel around here? Is it safe to walk the streets? It was a useful technique. The guy happily told her everything he knew about the area. We moved over to a slip and changed into our most touristy looking clothes.

We walked hand in hand up the beach, until we found the place called Ramone's. It had a rickety dock sticking out into the bay. Crude slips lined either side of it. I saw the pirate's boat. I immediately noticed that the outboard was in the down position, which gave me an idea. I whispered to Brody.

"The prop's in the water," I said. "We come back with a wrench and take it off."

"Just like that?"

"We'll dinghy over here," I said. "Snorkel around a bit. Keep our eyes open. When the coast is clear I'll sneak over and steal the prop. They won't even know it's missing until they try to leave."

"I like it," she said. "Much easier than trying to booger the engine somehow. Stay low in the water and no one will notice you."

We walked further up the beach before cutting over to a surface street. We walked back to the marina without encountering anyone resembling the pirates. They must have been someplace where they could see Tommy's boat. We lowered the dinghy and rounded up some tools. I took a short piece of lumber to jam in the prop, so I could get the nut off without turning the blades. I'd done this a dozen times on my own motors, but never under the water. I was only a semi-capable diver. I just couldn't hold my breath for long. I grabbed two sets of snorkel gear and off we went.

I anchored near the pier that held the pirate boat. We put our snorkels on and paddled about. There wasn't much to see. Just two silly gringos floating around the bay. There was no movement on the pier. I slowly drifted away from Brody and towards the boat. Any onlooker would be much more interested in watching Brody's nice figure in a bathing suit than keeping tabs on me. I came up behind the boat, took a good breath, and went back under. I kept the snorkel just above the surface. I jammed the board in the prop and put the wrench on the nut. I yanked on the wrench with all I had. Nothing happened. It was hard to get enough leverage underwater. I stuck my head up and looked around. I couldn't see much. I listened for voices. I heard none. I made sure the wrench was on the nut good and tight and pulled myself up by the transom. I put one foot on the wrench and pushed hard. It budged. I slid back underwater to conceal myself. I gave it a second and tried again with my arms. It started moving, slowly at first, but it was coming loose. I twisted the nut completely off, letting it drop to the sand below. I tried to wrestle the prop off the shaft. It wouldn't budge.

I heard voices above. Someone was on the pier. I was still breathing through the snorkel. Then I heard Brody's voice from out in the water. She was trying to distract them. I hoped they were looking her way and swam underwater away from the pier. I went out into deeper water, then circled in her direction. She was standing in knee-deep water, showing off her bikini body. Her distraction worked perfectly. The only problem was I hadn't actually removed the prop. I was certain that it would fall off when they tried to move the boat. Either it would spin off when they put it in reverse to leave the slip, or it would be pushed off by the force of their forward motion. It had to fall off, one way or the other.

We climbed into the dinghy and hurried back to the marina. I fired up the engine and Brody untied the lines. The dockhand was confused by our sudden departure. We'd only been in the slip for a few hours. I hoped he wasn't connected to our pirates in any way. We left him standing there and motored out into open water. As soon as we were close enough, I hailed Holly on her preferred VHF channel.

"Prepare to dive," I said. "We're on our way. We should be clear."

"Should be?" Holly responded.

"Long story," I said. "Just get ready to do your thing."

The fenders and tires were still out alongside the rusty old shrimper. We pulled up and tossed lines to Holly and Tommy. Holly was in her wet suit and Tommy had a mesh basket hanging from the now extended outrigger.

"You sure we won't have any company?" asked Tommy.

"Ninety-nine percent sure," I said. "I took the prop nut off their outboard, but I couldn't actually get the prop off."

"It'll spin off," said Holly. "Let's go."

"They store it with the motor down in the water," I said. "It's corroded, but no way it stays on under torque."

"I'm going in," said Holly. "Keep me safe up here."

We gave each other the thumbs up sign. She was one brave woman and the best diver I'd ever seen. This wasn't her first rodeo. We had developed confidence in each other's abilities through our many experiences together. I had a slight twinge of regret until Brody spoke.

"What do we do while we wait?" she asked.

"Let's arm up," I said. "Get every weapon out here and plenty of ammo. Tommy, get me some binoculars."

He was busy lowering the basket and feeding out air hose to Holly.

"They're on the helm," he said.

Brody and I rounded up two shotguns and three pistols. We had a box of bullets and shells for each. I let her check the actions and load up while I climbed up on the roof with the binoculars. She was better with guns than I was and took better care of them than I did. I scanned the horizon in the direction of the beach.

After thirty minutes, the first basket load came up. It was heavy with gold coins, gold bars, and an assortment of silver trinkets. Tommy raised his hands in the air and roared like he'd just won the Superbowl. Brody's eyes got big. She held her hands over her mouth in disbelief.

"Wow," she said. "Just wow. I hadn't considered what a pile of treasure would look like. This is amazing."

"Open the hold," yelled Tommy.

I jumped down and helped Brody get the heavy lid off the hold. Tommy swung the basket over the gunnel, positioning it over the hold. Brody and I went in and guided it down.

We dumped its contents on the floor. It had to be a few hundred pounds worth of precious metal.

We rode the basket back up to the deck. Holly was in the water at the transom.

"We good up here?" she asked.

"Hold on," I said, picking up the binoculars.

I looked through the dusty lenses and saw a boat heading our way.

"Boat coming out," I said.

"Shit," said Holly. "What do we do?"

"Ninety-nine percent sure you said," Tommy grumbled.

I climbed back on the roof to get a better look. It was them, headed directly towards us.

"It's them," I said. "I don't know how, but it's them. Man the battle stations."

Brody helped Holly climb aboard. Tommy grabbed a shotgun. The ladies armed themselves with pistols. Brody tossed a shotgun up to me on the roof. I trained the binoculars on the pirates. They were within a mile of us when it happened. All forward progress halted. They were dead in the water.

"They've stopped," I told my crew. "The prop finally fell off."

All three of them cheered.

"How much more is down there," I asked Holly.

"A lot," she said. "But it's more scattered. It'll take me an hour to fill the basket again."

"Are you good to go?"

"You know me," she said. "Damn the torpedoes."

I put Brody on the roof with the binoculars to keep an eye on our unwelcome guests. I gave Tommy a hand with the gear. He was sweating profusely and he looked a little pale.

"You okay?" I asked him.

"Too much excitement," he said. "I got all worked up about the gold first, then those assholes showed up. I'll be all right as long as they don't get back underway."

"Another boat coming out," yelled Brody.

The basket hit bottom. Holly's air hose was already deployed. Tommy wiped sweat from his forehead and sat down in the lone shady spot on deck.

"I'm glad you're here," he said. "I don't think I'm going to be much help if they try to board us."

"They're headed for the pirates," yelled Brody. "Not coming our way, yet."

With Holly down below and Tommy out of commission, we only had two gunners aboard. I liked it better when there were four of us and three of them. Now they had an extra man, assuming he was armed. We were outnumbered four to two. I gave Tommy a bottle of water and climbed up on the roof with Brody. I handed her the second pistol.

"What's going on out there?" I asked.

"Looks like the second boat is taking the first one in tow. They've got a line across," she said. "You think he'll tow them to us?"

"This is their big chance," I said. "Today's the day for them."

"The last thing we need is to have to shoot people," she said. "I hope they don't try anything."

"If they get within fifty feet just fire a bunch of rounds at the boats," I said. "Try not to hit anyone. Maybe that will be enough to scare them off."

"And when they fire back?"

"If they fire on us, shoot to kill."

I looked at her eyes trying to gauge her reaction. I saw steely determination. Neither of us wanted to shoot anyone, but if the shit hit the fan, I could count on her. I'd feel better if Holly was up here with us. She'd been down a long time. I knew I could count on her too.

"They're starting the tow," said Brody.

"Which way?"

"Give them a minute," she said.

We watched the tow rope come tight. They paralleled us for a minute, then slowly turned in our direction.

"Coming our way," said Brody.

"Signal Holly," I told Tommy. "Get her up here."

He yanked the air hose a few times to get her attention. She surfaced a minute later.

"What's going on?" she asked.

"They called a buddy," I said. "He's towing them out to us."

"Fuck," she said. "Help me aboard."

I grabbed her arm and helped her over the transom.

"Tommy's not feeling so good," I told her. "Take his shotgun. We're going to hit the boats, not the people, when they get close. We don't want to shoot at them unless they shoot at us."

"If they shoot at me they're going to eat some buckshot," she said. "There's a few million bucks worth of gold down there in that basket."

"I'll start hauling it up," said Tommy.

"They're making some headway now," yelled Brody. "Getting closer."

"Leave the basket down there," I said. "Everyone get behind the gunnel."

"One hundred yards out," said Brody.

"Fire on my signal," I said. "We don't have to be accurate. Empty your weapons, get your head back down and reload."

"Fifty yards," Brody said.

I peeked up over the rail. I didn't see a weapon on the guy driving the tow boat. The guys on the disabled boat all held guns. They didn't handle them like an experienced shooter. They looked awkward, almost comical. I thought I saw fear on the face of one of them. They must have really been desperate to attempt a hijack.

They were about fifty feet off our starboard side. The towing vessel turned to bring them alongside.

"Now!"

Holly, Brody and I blasted away at the boat hulls until we ran out of rounds.

"Down! Reload!"

The three pirates all dropped to the deck. I didn't think they'd been hit. They were just trying to gain some cover. The tow boat guy cut the rope and hauled ass towards shore. The disabled boat had drifted to within twenty feet of us.

"Throw your weapons overboard and we'll spare your lives," I yelled.

"Why you be shooting at us, man? We broke down. Just looking for a little help."

"Bullshit," I said.

I aimed my shotgun at the center console and pulled the trigger. His fish finder exploded.

"Toss the weapons, now," I yelled.

Three arms came up and plopped guns into the water.

"Stand up. Hands up," I commanded.

They did as they were told. They saw me and two women pointing weapons at them. Their boat wouldn't go. They were at our mercy.

"I say we feed them to the sharks," said Holly. "Rat bastards."

I looked over at Brody. She had a pistol in each hand, pretending to shoot one after the other.

"Pow, pow, pow, pow."

"Please mister, don't shoot us. We can't do nothing to hurt you now. We'll just float away, call for help later. You go on about your business. Just don't kill us."

They were indeed floating away from us. A light breeze was pushing them slowly towards shore.

"Just keep floating," I said. "Don't call for help. You'll make it to shore sometime tonight I figure. If the wind doesn't change."

The leader looked around. He put his finger in his mouth before putting it up in the air.

He seemed satisfied that they were indeed heading towards the beach.

"If we ain't gonna make it, I'll have to call somebody," he said.

"If you come back out here, there won't be any warning shots," I said. "And I'll shoot you first."

"No need for no more shooting," he said. "Won't see us again."

My crew gathered by my side. We watched the pathetic pirates drift farther and farther away.

"The basket is still down there," said Holly. "Let's bring it up and blow this popcorn stand."

Tommy looked a little better, but when he moved towards the winch controls I stopped him.

"Take it easy," I said. "Holly can run this. Me and Brody can get it in the hold."

He sat back in the shade and nodded agreement.

"You need to fill the hold with sea water when you're done," he said. "Keeps the silver from corroding until we can clean it up."

The basket broke the surface. A little rainbow appeared in the water running off the gold. The sun lit up our treasure in a gold and silver glow. It was a magnificent sight that few on earth had ever seen. I could appreciate why Tommy had never given up in his quest for treasure. He was already rich, but this was his drug. Now Holly would be rich too. I couldn't be happier for them. Holly brought the boom over the hold and lowered the basket. Brody and I dumped its contents.

"We could literally bathe in gold," said Brody. "Or make gold angels. I had no idea."

"Quite the haul," I said. "I'm sure Tommy will give us a cut if you want some of it."

"Maybe just a nice medallion for a necklace," she said. "We're still good for money aren't we?"

"We're fine," I said. "But if Tommy insists on paying us, I'm not saying no."

We helped Holly stow away the gear and get it secured. She turned on the pumps to fill the hold with sea water. The pirates had drifted out of sight. Our work day was done. Tommy was looking much better. We were all smiles.

"I'll grab some beers off my boat," I said.

"I've got a case of champagne that I've been saving for this day," said Tommy. "Everybody gets their own bottle."

We each grabbed a bottle and started working on the cork.

"Wait," I said. "A few words, please. To Tommy, for his knowledge, skill and gold-sniffing instincts."

"Here, here!" said the crew.

"To Holly, for her ridiculous diving ability, physical prowess, fearlessness, and unending determination."

"Here, here!"

"God bless this rusty old ship too," I said. "Congratulations to the best damn treasure hunters on the planet. You two deserve this. I'm proud to know you both."

"My turn," said Holly. "To Breeze, who has the uncanny ability to show up out of the blue at the most opportune times. I think he smelled this gold all the way from Florida. We couldn't have done it without you, seriously. My never ending thanks to you and Brody."

"You're entitled to a chunk of this," said Tommy.

"We've haven't sold it yet," I said.

"You'll stick around and help with that too, won't you?" he asked.

"For right now, I say we pull up anchor and get away from this place," I said. "We don't want those guys coming back out here with a small army."

"He's right," said Holly. "Let's beat feet."

"Where to?" I asked.

"My contact is in Belize City," said Tommy. "Let's cross into Guatemalan waters and hole up near Punta Gorda. We'll figure out our next step from there."

The girls were standing there holding unopened bottles of champagne.

"Cheers!" I said.

Corks went flying in four different directions. Holly poured half her bottle over her head. Brody spit champagne laughing at her. Holly dumped the rest of her bottle over Brody's head, then stole Brody's bottle and took a long swig. I entertained a brief fantasy about me and two champagne covered cuties. I raised my bottle to take a drink, but Brody got her bottle back and dumped it on me. Both girls thought this was hilarious. I managed to get a drink.

"Fuck it," I said, pouring the rest of my bottle over my head.

We all laughed our asses off. It was a giddy time. We ended up sharing Tommy's bottle until it too was empty. We tossed them all in the sea. It was time to go.

Five

Our vessels were at anchor on the ocean side of Punta Gorda, in Guatemala. Brody and I had joined Holly and Tommy aboard the shrimper for dinner and discussion. Tommy's first priority was to clean and catalog the treasure. With his vast experience he could come up with a good estimate of its value.

"Let me ask you two a question," I said, addressing Tommy and Holly. "How did you think you were going to get that stuff up off the bottom without any help?"

"We tried hiring locals to stand guard for us," Holly said. "But they couldn't hack it out there for weeks at a time. They'd quit as soon as we got to shore."

"And we weren't real sure they'd be much help if something ever did happen," said Tommy.

"We didn't have anything to bring up until last week," said Holly. "The pirates started showing up after we stayed in one spot for a while."

"On top of the gold," I said. "Then Brody and I showed up. Problem solved."

"Serendipity for you," said Holly. "A godsend for us."

"Glad we could help," I said. "Can we call it even now? I'd like to think I'm square with both of you now."

"I'm good," said Tommy. "I'm still paying you both for your part in this."

Holly crossed her arms and thought about it for a minute. She stood up and walked over to me, looking directly into my eyes. We still had a deep connection, even though we were no longer a couple.

"I don't know what happened to you back there in Texan Bay," she said. "But I'm going to try to forget it ever happened. I won't let one brief moment erase all that we've meant to each other. You shouldn't either. If you'll help us turn that gold into cash, I'll be forever in your debt."

I looked at Brody.

"I don't know exactly what we're getting into," she said. "But I'll help however I can. Breeze?"

The job was only half done. There wasn't much point in bailing out after we'd come this far.

"We're going to need a solid plan," I said. "I'm not winging it this time. Who are we dealing with?"

"Right now we talk to a guy, who talks to another guy, who then talks to our potential buyer," said Tommy.

"We need to get straight to the source," I said. "Who is he? Is he a mobster? Cartel guy? Kingpin?"

"He's a broker of rare collectibles," said Tommy. "A business man."

"So he's a middleman who takes his cut of the profits," I said.

"That's the only way that Tommy can sell," said Holly. "His name is toxic in the precious metals trade."

"Plus we can't let the governments of Belize or Mexico get wind of the deal," said Tommy. "We'll be in court for years. Obviously, I can't do that."

"So we let the middle man cut our take," I said. "How much will he ding us for?"

"Probably half," said Tommy. "We'll still get millions."

"Drain the hold tomorrow and start figuring out just what we've got," I said. "Get me in touch with your first contact. I'll see if I can't buy my way past him to the second guy."

"Get this," said Holly. "The broker calls himself Juan Valdez."

"Probably not his real name," I said. "Maybe he likes coffee beans, I don't know. Is he from Belize or Mexico?"

"He's Columbian," said Tommy. "Speaks perfect American English. Wears expensive suits. Enjoys the finer things."

"So you have done some research," I said.

"A little," he said. "I got kind of wrapped up in the recovery mode."

"This sounds like a job for Winston Shade," said Holly.

"Who's Winston Shade?" asked Brody.

Holly laughed before explaining my alter ego to Brody.

"Breeze is Winston Shade," said Brody. "I think I might like seeing him in an Italian suit."

"He'll need a haircut too," said Holly. "We'll give him a makeover. Mani-pedi and facial."

The two of them giggled like school girls.

"Where do we get nice clothes down here?" I asked.

"There are marinas in Belize City," said Tommy. "Lots of shops there."

"Do you have a phone, Brody?" asked Holly.

"Yes, but it's useless right now," she answered.

"You can get a SIM card there too," Holly said. "You two go up there while we go through the gold. Turn Breeze into Winston and make contact with the first guy. See what happens."

"It's a start," I said. "Give us a few days, maybe a week."

"It will take that long to clean and count everything," said Tommy.

We were all on the same wavelength. We all had a job to do. We were four very unique individuals working as one. It felt good, even though I knew it would end soon. Brody and I couldn't hang out with Holly for too long. We'd get this deal done and resume our trip towards Florida. It would be nice to go back home. The extra cash wouldn't hurt either. It amused me how I'd once again stumbled into good fortune. Mostly I'd stumbled into lion's dens and snake pits. This time it felt different. Maybe Brody had changed my luck.

I got a quick rundown on Belize City from Tommy before we left. He told me that the anchorage had poor holding and was often rolly. He suggested Cucumber Beach Marina, just off the Western Highway. It was five miles from town but cabs were readily available. None of the other marinas were deep enough for us to enter.

"Watch out for cruise ships coming and going," he said. "And watch out for pickpockets and such when on land. Don't go out at night. Stay alert."

"Sounds divine," said Brody.

"It's fine during the day," said Tommy. "Just be aware of your personal safety at all times."

"Breeze tells me that all the time," she said. "I think he forgets what I did for a living."

"I forget a lot of things when I see you in a bikini," I said.

Brody and I ran up the coast the next day. We had to anchor outside the marina entrance to wait for high tide. Even then, we barely made it in. The staff was friendly and professional. They called for Customs to check us in. It was a painless process.

We got a cab to take us into town. After a quick bite, we went shopping. We got the fancy suit and all the fancy accessories to go with it. The next day I suffered through a salon haircut. Brody got a SIM card for her phone. Just like that, we were ready.

I called the first guy in the communication chain. He didn't want to meet in person, but the promise of a crisp one hundred dollar bill changed his mind. We arranged to meet at a little restaurant called Nerie's, on Daly Street. It looked like a dump from outside but was actually neat and clean inside. The food smelled great. Our guest arrived right on time. He called himself Don. It didn't take him long to ask for the money I'd promised.

"I want to meet the person that you talk to, who talks with Juan Valdez," I said.

"I don't know if that is possible," he said. "This arrangement is to keep Mr. Valdez isolated from the dirty work."

"I am not a man of the street," I said. "And what I'd really like is a meeting with Mr. Valdez himself."

"No," he said. "That is not possible."

"Listen," I said. "I have a multi-million dollar proposal for him. It's his line of work. He'll want to talk to me."

"I don't talk to him," he explained. "I have never even met the man."

"But you know someone who has," I said. "Get me in touch with him."

Don muttered and fumbled around with his hands. I peeled off five more hundreds from a gold money clip and slipped them across the table. I will give the same to your friend if he will meet with me.

"I will ask," he said. "How will I get in touch with you?"

I gave him Brody's cell number. He pushed his chair back and stood up.

"It is not wise to show such amounts of cash on the street in this city," he said.

"I understand," I said. "Thank you for your time. We'll wait for your call."

We walked back to the marina via a circuitous route. I watched for a tail. I detected no one following us. Brody was doing the same thing. She didn't sense anyone watching us either. Don was a low-level man in the operation. I'd just paid him more than he made in a month. The closer we got to the big man, the more careful we'd have to be.

He called the next day. The number two man in the chain of communication was not interested in a meeting. He was not in the habit of wasting Mr. Valdez's time. Five hundred dollars was not enough incentive to change his mind. I insisted on speaking with Don in person. We met in a park just north of the downtown area.

"Maybe if you had some references he could verify," said Don. "Add another five hundred to your offer."

"Listen to me, Don," I began. "I don't need any references. I'm Winston Shade, a big player in South Florida politics, but that's not why I'm here."

"Maybe if you told us what it is you wish to accomplish," he said. "Maybe he will listen, I can't say."

"Spanish gold," I said. "From a shipwreck. Coins, bars, silver too. Many millions."

Don raised an eyebrow and scratched his chin.

"I will pass this information along," he said. "I think Mr. Valdez would want to know about this."

"Thank you," I said, slipping him one gold coin. "A small sample, for you to keep."

"Many millions?" he asked.

"That's right."

"I will call you again tomorrow."

The next day's call was more promising. Valdez's number two had agreed to meet. I was instructed to wait in the park where I'd spoken with Don. He kept me waiting for thirty minutes.

"Mr. Shade, I presume," the man said. He was tall with dark hair, nicely groomed. He wore a nice suit, with expensive looking shoes. He introduced himself as Hector.

"Winston Shade," I said. "Thanks for agreeing to speak with me."

"Time is money, Mr. Shade," he said. "Let's not waste it."

"I represent the world's premier treasure hunter," I explained. "He prefers to keep the sale of his latest find under the radar. He's already quite wealthy, so he's willing to accept something below face value, in order to maintain his anonymity. It's a golden opportunity for someone with the resources to buy and sell such a thing."

"What is the approximate value of this find?" he asked.

"We've got a team cataloging the treasure as we speak," I said. "They should have a final count within a few days."

"Ballpark me," he said.

"Rough estimate at best," I said. "Five hundred pounds at today's twelve hundred per ounce is just shy of ten million dollars. Not counting historic value or intrinsic worth to collectors."

"Mr. Valdez has several clients who are always on the lookout for these types of precious metals. Just when you think the last of the Peruvian and Columbian gold has been found, someone finds another ship," he said. "But he won't make a purchase without already coming to terms with a buyer. You understand?"

"It's a lot of cash to have laying around," I said. "I understand."

"I will need a complete itemization of every piece," he said. "I will need samples as evidence of this find. Any hint of fraud will end our negotiations. Contact me through Don when you are prepared."

"I still want to meet with Mr. Valdez," I said. "I like to take the measure of a man when I'm negotiating."

"It is my job to take your measure, Mr. Shade," he said. "But this mystery treasure hunter won't present himself."

"You are the intermediary for Valdez," I said. "I'm doing the same for my guy."

"We don't even have his name," he said. "I can assure you it will remain confidential. These relationships can be fragile I know, but if he's as famous as you claim, Mr. Valdez will know of him."

I thought about it for a minute. I knew that Tommy wanted to stay a ghost, but I was getting somewhere with this quest to find a buyer. Sure, Valdez would know of him. I decided that greed would win the day. He'd be more interested in selling Tommy's gold than turning Tommy in.

"It's Tommy Thompson," I said. "He hired me to make a deal. That's why I'm here and he's not."

"An interesting turn of events," said Hector. "I speculate that Mr. Valdez will be happy to be a part of this transaction, but I can't speak for him."

"I'll get you the list and valuation," I said. "Tell him to start finding a buyer."

"Good day, Mr. Shade," he said.

"Good day."

When I got back to the marina, there was a ruckus going on. Brody, wearing a bikini, had some local guy by his little finger. He was on his knees on the dock, begging for mercy. His buddies were laughing at his expense.

"What the hell, Brody?" I said. "Leave you alone for one hour and you're beating up the neighbors."

"He forgot the look but don't touch rule," she said. "Thought it would be fun to grab my ass."

"Learn your lesson, amigo?" I asked the poor guy.

"She's breaking my finger," he cried. "Please, I'm sorry."

"Let go of him, Brody," I said. "He's had enough."

She dropped her grip on him and gave him a swift kick in the ass as he tried to stand. He stumbled forward and fell off the dock. This caused his buddies to break out into a fit of raucous laughter. The guy in the water was not so amused.

"Come on," I said to Brody. "Let's toss the lines and get out of here."

"What's up?" she asked.

"I've got to get a good count of what Tommy and Holly have for a potential buyer."

"That's great news," she said. "Things are moving fast."

"I still haven't talked to Valdez," I told her. "But I think he'll deal. We've got to convince him that we're legit."

"Let's roll then," she said. "Fire her up and I'll get the lines."

We bumped bottom attempting to leave the marina. *Miss Leap's* big prop churned up mud as we struggled to push through the shallows.

I was relieved when we finally made deeper water. I didn't want to be stuck with those local guys still hanging around, or embarrassed because I hadn't checked the tide before leaving.

The run down the coast was an easy one. We found Tommy's old shrimper in the same spot. When we arrived in the dinghy, Tommy and Holly popped their heads up from the hold.

"Come on down," yelled Holly. "We're just about done here."

They'd sorted the coins and bars, both gold and silver into different containers. I saw milk crates, cardboard boxes, ammo cans, and burlap sacks all filled with loot. Tommy was flipping through a clipboard full of yellow legal paper.

"I still gotta research some of these different coins," he said. "But you're looking at five hundred and forty-two pounds of gold alone. Ten point four million in raw gold value. Another million, give or take, in silver."

Holly did a little dance around the containers.

"I'm a hippie millionaire," she exclaimed. "A dread-locked blondie rich bitch."

Her smile was worth a million bucks. Even crusty old Tommy was smiling.

"You done good, kid," he said to Holly. "You done real good."

"Breeze has some good news," said Brody. "Or should I say Winston?"

"I didn't get to Valdez," I said. "But I got to his number two. Seemed real interested in working a deal. They need an itemized list of every piece, and some samples to go with it."

"I got it all right here," said Tommy. "Maybe one of the girls can tidy up my handwriting, but it's all there."

"Good job, Breeze," said Holly. "You're a pretty handy guy sometimes."

"It's not a done deal, yet," I said.

"Shit works out," she said. "You'll make it happen."

There we were, the four of us standing amongst unbelievable riches. We were all smiling. Brody suggested we take the party up on deck and add some alcohol. I concurred. We sat in the refreshing Caribbean breeze and drank Belikin beers. We played a game of "What to do with the money." Tommy would remain anonymous and under cover, but he suggested that his treasure hunting days were over. It was time to enjoy his success. Brody and I wouldn't be as rich as the other two, but we'd enjoy a continued life of leisure without financial worry. Holly was the only one with big plans.

"I'm going to outfit *Another Adventure* for world cruising," she proclaimed. "You'll hear my name in every tropic port between here and New Zealand."

I gave Brody a light squeeze. Holly was no longer my first priority. Soon she'd be gone for good. I wished her well.

Six

Back in Belize City, I made the call to Don. He got back to me within the hour. Hector would come to my boat to see the samples that very evening. He was bringing Valdez. Brody had re-written Tommy's inventory list in pleasant feminine handwriting. The samples we'd brought with us had been cleaned and polished to a high sheen. We kept them in velvet Crown Royal bags.

"Have we got everything together?" asked Brody. "Are we missing anything?"

"We're ready on our end," I told her. "This isn't the hairy part. We'll need to arrange for a safe exchange of goods for cash if things go well. That's when it gets risky."

"How do you want it to go down?" she asked.

"I'm still working it out," I said. "I'll have a better idea after I meet this Valdez character."

"See what your gut tells you?" she asked.

"My gut, my eyes, my ears, even my nose," I said. "He's supposed to be a businessman, but that doesn't mean he won't resort to violence. Al Capone was a businessman too."

"And we're dealing in a third world country," she said.

"I want you to sit in on the discussion," I said. "Be open to your intuition. We'll compare notes later."

"How come when it involves a man it's called situational awareness like it's some special skill?" she asked. "But when it's a woman it's called intuition?"

"Intuition is the feminine word for gut feeling," I said. "We're a team. We need to use all of the skills that we have at our disposal."

"I'll watch the man like a hawk," she said. "I'll notice any tic or tell."

It was after dark before we saw Hector coming down the dock with another man. I granted them permission to board and made the introductions. Valdez was small in stature but very formal with his posture. He wore a pitch black mane of hair like a lion. He had the features of an Incan or Mayan. His handshake was firm and dry. He looked me in the eye. He managed a faint smile when introduced to Brody. I saw him shoot Hector a glance of disapproval.

"I wasn't told of a female partner," said Valdez. "I would have brought a small gift."

"Thank you but it's not necessary," said Brody. "Nice to meet you."

We all sat around the salon table where the velvet bags were. I handed each one of the pieces to Valdez as Brody read from the inventory list. The gold coins were not all uniform in shape or size, but each had been weighed. Valdez examined each one carefully. When he was finished he gave them to Hector, who put them in a brief case. The process went on for almost an hour.

"May I also examine the itemized list? Asked Valdez.

Brody turned it over, minus the total values that Tommy had calculated. When he finished flipping through the pages, he handed the list to Hector. It went into the briefcase too.

"It will take some time to ascertain the value of this find," said Valdez.

"I've got the raw metal values right here," I said. "We're not particularly interested in the historic worth or how much of a premium a collector would be willing to pay. That's your concern. We're looking for quick cash."

"You're not much of a negotiator, Mr. Breeze," he said. "I expected something different."

"I'm being honest and upfront with you," I said. "I'm hoping for the same from you."

"Have you participated in similar transactions previously?" he asked.

"I have, but under different circumstances," I said. "I played hardball and made the exchange with superior firepower and strength. I'd like to avoid that this time."

I saw a quick twitch of his eye. I'd said something unexpected. I don't think he liked the unpredictable. He shot a quick glance at Hector.

"I'm not sure what kind of a hand you are holding," he said. "I could certainly raise the firepower stakes if necessary, but I find it distasteful."

"Then why don't we all leave the guns at home?" I said.

"My men will be armed," he said. "The treasure will need to be protected, but we can remain civilized, can we not?"

"The civility which money will purchase is rarely extended to those who have none," I said.

"Charles Dickens," he said. "And I will have the money."

"Make us an offer," I said. "Be straight up. Don't dick us around."

He asked for the raw metals value of our treasure, assuring me that he would verify the information with his own sources. I told him we figured it to be eleven and a half million dollars.

"I'll pay fifty cents on the dollar," he said.

"That's five and three-quarter million," I said. "Make it an even six and you've got a deal."

"Six million dollars," he said. "This transaction will turn out to be very lucrative for me."

"Keep that in mind when we make the exchange," I said. "You'll make millions. No point in shooting the guy who set it up for you."

"Is the rest of it here, on this boat?" he asked.

"Of course not," I said. "It's not even in this country. We'll need time to transport it to a meeting place."

"Wise decision," he said. "I'll have Hector call you with the details."

"Look me in the eye and tell me this will go down smoothly, with no one getting hurt," I said.

He turned to face me squarely and looked me in the eye.

"I cannot make a promise that may be affected by your behavior, or that of your people," he said. "My men will do what is necessary to retrieve the product. If you keep your people in line, you'll get the money as discussed. I wish you no ill will, but if this turns sour, I will rain all of Hell down upon you."

"It won't go sour due to us," I said. "All we want is a smooth and fair exchange. If you screw it up, maybe I'll rain a little Hell of my own."

"Enough posturing," he said. "Wait for Hector's call. Deliver the goods."

"Have a nice evening, Mr. Valdez," I said.

He stood, gave a nod to Brody, and walked out of the salon. Hector hung back.

"You are leaving a few million dollars on the table in this deal," he said. "But that will only generate so much good will. Just do as we say and everything will be fine."

"I intend to," I said. "You keep Valdez from harming us in exchange."

"I will get his assurance before I call," he said. "I'll be getting a nice finder's fee if we are successful."

"Good for you," I said. "Let's make it happen."

Brody and I put our heads together after they left. She'd noticed a few things that I hadn't.

When I'd mentioned firepower and superior strength, Hector noticeably flinched. I'd been focused on Valdez. Both had indicated surprise at the notion of me bringing the heat to the exchange. They'd underestimated me. The problem now was the fact that I had very little firepower to bring.

"Valdez was disturbed that he didn't know about me," said Brody. "He doesn't like surprises."

"He didn't soften in the presence of your beauty either," I said. "He's all business."

"What's your gut telling you?"

"I think he'll bring tough men with big guns," I said. "But that's just insurance. He wants the gold. We'll get our money."

"I agree about ninety percent," she said. "The other ten percent of me wonders what happens when they just take the gold and don't pay up."

"We'll have to come up with a plan for that ten percent possibility," I said.

"Looks like we'll have a few days to think about it," she said.

"Let's get back to Holly and Tommy," I said. "It's their money after all."

Leap of Faith was getting familiar with the coast of Belize. I was thinking that I'd be glad when the mission was over, so we could make progress towards Florida. I was also thinking that we needed to find a place to do some maintenance before crossing big water. An oil change was coming due soon. We chugged southward at seven knots, enjoying the ride. We dropped anchor near the old shrimper late that afternoon. Holly's voice came over the radio.

"Get over here," she said. "Dying to hear how it went."

We took the dinghy over to them and climbed aboard.

"Six million dollars," said Brody. "Breeze is the six million dollar man."

"Holy shit!" said Holly. "Is this really happening?"

"We still have to make the exchange," I said.

"What's your take on this guy?" asked Tommy.

"For the most part, we agree that it will be straight forward," I said.

"But?"

"But there's a slight chance it won't," I said. "We need to prepare for that."

"If they bring any kind of force at all," said Brody. "We'll be sitting ducks. We can't outgun them."

"Two chicks, an old man, and Breeze," said Tommy. "These won't be local pirates we're dealing with."

"We need a contingency," I said. "We'll assume it goes fine, but have something ready for them if it doesn't."

"Like what?" Holly asked.

"Don't know yet," I said. "We'll get to the drop off site early. I'll look around and figure something out."

"I thought we weren't winging it this time," said Holly.

"There are too many variables," I said. "I'll come up with something when I get a look at the place."

Holly and Brody looked at each other and shrugged. I told them not to worry. Secretly, I was worried enough for all four of us. I found a way to put my friends at risk yet again. Or maybe they'd found a way to put me at risk. Either way, we were in it together. I couldn't afford to let them down, they were the only real friends I had. Shit would have to work out.

It was three days before we got the call from Hector. He wanted to do the transfer at the same marina we'd visited in Ambergris Caye. There was simply not enough room for Tommy's shrimp boat in there, so we'd have to transfer the treasure to *Leap of Faith*. I was to call him when we were tied up in a slip for further instructions.

"Do you have a feel for Valdez's intentions?" I asked. "We're not walking into an ambush are we?"

"Remain calm and do as you're told," he said. "You'll get the money. No tricks, you understand?"

"I got it," I told him. "Stay calm. Do as we're told."

We loaded the loot into the bilge of my boat. Tommy and Holly packed overnight bags and joined us. Four's a crowd on *Miss Leap*, but we were all used to cramped conditions. Brody cleaned and checked our meager armory. Tommy plopped himself on the settee to rest. Holly helped me get underway. It was a simple matter to follow the GPS bread crumbs back to Belize.

"This is real convenient for me," said Holly. "*Another Adventure* is in the same marina. I'll be glad to get back to her."

"Can you get Tommy back to his boat after this is over?" I asked. "Brody and I are really itching to get back to Florida."

"Of course," she said. "I owe him a lot."

"He couldn't have done it without you," I said.

"Yet, you show up to put the finishing touches on the whole thing," she said. "I still can't get over it."

"You're welcome," I said.

"Thanks, Breeze."

We gave each other knowing looks. We'd been through a lot together. It was drawing close to the end for us. There were new chapters to be written in our lives, but they wouldn't include each other. We cruised on in silence until Brody joined us on the bridge.

"I've been thinking," she said. "We already know the layout of the marina. We can start working on a plan."

"There's a squeeze point where the main pier attaches to land," I said. "That's where we hit them if it goes bad."

"Hit them with what?" asked Holly. "If you and Brody are on the boat, it will just be Tommy and me."

"Some kind of booby trap?" I said. "Trip wire maybe. Surprise will be on our side. They don't know you two are with us."

"Don't call Hector until we have a plan of action sorted out," said Brody.

Tommy wasn't with us to speak for himself, but I didn't think he'd be much use. I'd have to send Brody ashore with Holly. That was my last line of defense, two pretty women. I didn't like it. I quietly prayed that Hector's assurance would come true. I'd just hand over the goods and get the cash. The girls could stand down. Valdez's men would leave. No one would get hurt.

I turned my attention to navigation and gauge watching. All were within normal parameters. That oil change needed to happen sooner rather than later. To distract myself, I played with the GPS, plotting our way back to Florida. If we jumped off from Mexico, we could make it to Grand Cayman without running out of fuel. One last long jump from there to Florida and we'd be home.

Seven

We tied up in a slip at the marina in Ambergris. As soon as we stepped foot on land, we encountered the three pirates we'd disarmed and sent packing. Everyone stopped in their tracks. An idea came to me.

"We didn't expect to see you again," said the big one. "What did you do with that rusty old shrimper?"

"It's far away from here, amigo," I said. "Let's be friends, eh? I have a proposition for you."

"What kind of proposition?" he asked.

"Cash money for muscle," I said. "Just backup really. Probably nothing will happen at all, but you'll still get paid."

"Paid to do what?" he asked. "And how much?"

"I will have some visitors," I said. "If all goes well, they will simply leave. If not, we will hit them hard, right there at the end of that pier. These two ladies will be behind you with weapons, concealed."

"Why should we help you?"

"For starters, because I didn't kill you out there on the water," I said. "And for money. You like money don't you?"

"Again, how much?"

"I'll give each of you one hundred dollars right now," I said. "You'll get another hundred after the deal is done. I'll even throw in some cold beer. We'll set you up under that tiki when the time comes."

"Let's see the cash," he said.

I pulled three big bills out of my pocket and handed them to him. He looked at his buddies. They nodded in agreement. He gave each of them a hundred.

"When do we show up?" he asked.

"Tomorrow evening around six," I said. "I'll have the beer on ice."

"Gracias," he said. "We'll be here."

After they were gone we surveyed the grounds. We found spots for my army of two to hide. We'd send Tommy into town to avoid any trouble.

"How can we be sure our new friends will act when we need them?" asked Brody.

"We give them a clear impetus to move," I said. "Set up a trip wire here at the end of the pier. Take down the first guy off the dock. The others will be limited for space. Our guys pile on before they can draw their weapons. Remember, they'll be carrying a heavy load. You two pop out with guns drawn. I come from behind them. It's over."

"It might work," said Brody. "But these men won't be easy marks. It's dangerous."

"Let's all hope it doesn't come to that," I said. "But prepare like it will."

"How do you make a trip wire," asked Holly.

"Hell if I know," I said. "Let's go up to the ship's store and look around."

We walked the aisles and poked around. I picked up some thin cable used for safety line on sailboats. Brody found some little pulleys. Holly showed us how to use a crimping tool to put loops on the ends. Between the three of us, we manufactured a rig that would work. I screwed the pulleys into dock pilings about crotch high. We ran the cable through some mangroves to where Brody would be hiding. I stuffed the cable down in the gap between two dock boards. It would be invisible in the dark. We tried it out a couple of times and it worked smoothly.

"Remember," I said. "Yank it hard and fast at the last possible second. Then come running."

"I got it," said Brody.

"Don't shoot the three amigos," I said. "Don't shoot at all if you can help it."

After checking on Tommy, I called Hector. I told him that everything was ready for the transfer. His men would arrive soon after dark. I went and bought beer for our hired hands. I put them in a cooler in the shade of the tiki. They arrived right on time, smiling and laughing. This would be the easiest money they ever made. Getting paid to drink beer is a good gig if you can get it. If everything went to hell, though, they'd be sorry they accepted this job.

We sent Tommy to a restaurant in town with instructions not to move until someone came for him. He apologized for not being able to help. He looked old and tired.

"It will all be over soon," I assured him.

"Good luck," he said.

Holly and Brody helped me bring the treasure up into the salon of *Leap of Faith*. I had to assume that the men coming later would bring something to haul it in. If I got the money, I'd drag it up the dock myself if need be. Then we huddled under the tiki for last minute instructions and encouragement. The leader of the three amigos handed us each a beer.

"Everyone just sit still and quiet when they arrive," I said. "I've worked out some signals to let you know what's going on."

"What kind of signals?" Holly asked.

"Lights and a horn," I said. "If all is well, meaning I got the money, I'll turn on the anchor light. White light means all is right."

"And if they ripped us off?" asked Brody.

"Nav lights, red and green," I answered. "Red and green is bad. Proceed to take them out."

"What if you can't signal us?" asked Holly. "God forbid."

"I'll keep that canned air horn within arm's reach," I said. "If you hear the air horn, I'm down and need immediate help. Come running with guns blazing."

Brody went back over the signals.

"White is all right," she said. "Red and Green is bad. Horn is very bad."

"That's it," I said. "Everybody got it?"

They all nodded.

"It won't be long now," I said. "Everyone take your position. Say a little prayer maybe."

I went back to the boat alone. I cracked the blinds a little so I could peek out. Darkness fell and I kept telling myself to keep calm. *Just be cool, Breeze. It'll work out.*

Four large men appeared at the top of the pier. Two were wheeling big pieces of luggage. Two held duffel bags. They paused and looked around cautiously before proceeding down the dock. I met them on the port side where I wanted them to board. The first one stood over me on the finger pier and opened his jacket to reveal his sidearm. I motioned him aboard. The two guys with the wheeled luggage had a hard time fitting their load on the narrow side deck. I almost panicked when I thought they wouldn't fit, but they barely squeezed by. Eventually, we all stood in the salon. Their expressions were grim, angry even. They were alert and kept their hands near their weapons. One of them went back outside to stand guard. If they decided to take me out and leave with the gold I was toast. I uncovered the containers of loot.

"Feel free to take a look," I said. "I personally verify that it will match the inventory list exactly."

The duffel bags were opened. They were full of cash.

"Feel free to take a look," one of them said. "We'll verify that it's all there."

I moved slowly to the bags. I picked them up and hefted them. This was no time to count money. I nodded, zipped up the bags, and tossed them down into the lower berth. I waved my arms over the treasure.

"It's all yours," I said.

That's when the guns came out. Three mean looking, badass dudes stood there pointing mean looking weapons at me.

"Load it into the luggage," one of them told me.

Another man checked outside with the lookout. All was quiet outside. I started loading silver and gold. I pictured Brody crouched down in the mangroves with her hand on the trip wire. I could see Holly squeezing her weapon, ready to shoot if necessary. I was so close to making her rich, I was sure she could taste it.

I was uncomfortable not being in control of the situation, but I had no choice but to follow out their orders. I built up a sweat lugging coins and bars into the luggage. The men stood rock still, pointing their guns.

"Hurry up," I was told.

I hurried. When I was done, all three men used their guns to direct me into the lower berth. I went down the steps and stood with the bags of money. If they were going to shoot me, then was the time. My shotgun was under the mattress to my right, but I didn't dare reach for it. I was too far from the air horn to sound it. I'd forgotten all about it. They let me stand there for a full minute, sweating and fretting. Two of them turned to the luggage and started carting it off. The third kept his gun trained on me. I could hear them struggling to squeeze the now full luggage through the narrow side deck. When I heard it clunk up onto the pier, the last guy turned and left the salon. I could feel his weight leave the boat when he climbed off. The wheels on the luggage made a clacking sound as they rolled up the dock towards land.

I flipped on the anchor light. White is all right. I went out the back door and looked up, but couldn't see the light. I quickly clamored to the bow and looked up again. It wasn't lit. Clack, clack, clack went the luggage. I ran back inside and wiggled the switch. It didn't work. On the way back out I grabbed a flashlight. I climbed the stairs to the bridge, grabbed a cooler, and hoisted myself as high as I could get. I turned on the flashlight, first pointing it at the non-functioning anchor light, then towards shore. I waved it frantically. God, I hoped that Brody could see it. If she pulled the tripwire now, there would be hell to pay. I had not turned on the nav lights. There was no red and green signal. *Don't do it, Brody.*

The clacking stopped. The men had made it off the pier and onto solid land. The three amigos sat drinking beer under the tiki. Holly and Brody sat swatting mosquitoes in their hiding spots. All of us watched as the luggage rolled to a waiting SUV. A collective sigh of relief went up when it drove away. The girls emerged from their lairs.

"What the fuck was that?" said Holly.

"Jesus Christ, Breeze," said Brody. "I wasn't sure what to do."

"You did the right thing," I said. "We've got the money. The deal is done."

"Wahoo!" yelled Holly, waking the neighborhood. "Six million mofuggin dollars."

"I guess so," I said. "I didn't count it."

"Let's go see it," she said.

I tossed the duffel bags up into the salon and the girls attacked them with vigor. They each grabbed stacks of bills and waved them around. I stood between them and they both hugged me, still holding wads of cash. A quick picture flashed through my mind. All of us were naked and rolling around in the money, fulfilling the threesome fantasy amidst a mountain of hundred dollar bills. Then I remembered Tommy and the three amigos.

I went up to the tiki and handed out three more hundreds. My pirate friends were appreciative. I thanked them and shook hands with each of them.

"Take the beers to go," I said. "Hell, take the whole damn cooler if you want."

Holly and Brody came out and I went to retrieve Tommy. The girls stayed behind with the money. I found him slumped over on the bar. At first, I thought maybe he'd had a heart attack or something, but he was just sleeping. I paid his tab and helped him to his feet.

"We got it, old boy," I told him. "The deal is done. No one got hurt."

"Heck of a job, Breeze," he said. "I don't know how you do it, but thanks again."

"Shit works out, Tommy," I said. "Shit works out."

We went back to the boat and spent the rest of the night counting money.

Eight

We had three million in Holly's pile and three million in Tommy's. It was all there, exactly six million dollars. Tommy tried to give me and Brody a million bucks, but I wouldn't have it. We argued over it until I was forced to accept a half-million. Holly made an effort to force money on me too, but I won that argument. The two of them had spent a year looking for that treasure, using Tommy's gear and Holly's skills. I was a late-comer to the find. I was happy to help. I'd mostly made up for my earlier misdeeds. I felt better about leaving this way.

"So what's next for you two?" Holly asked.

"We want to head north right away," I said. "We'll need a day to re-supply. Plus I have to fix that anchor light."

"What about you and Tommy?" asked Brody.

"My boat is here," Holly answered. "I can get Tommy back to his."

"You might consider getting him to a doctor," said Brody.

"I'll be okay," said Tommy. "This stack of money has me feeling better. I think my days of high adventure are over though."

"I'll need a day to get my boat ready too," Holly said. "Let's meet tomorrow night for a send-off party."

Tommy and Holly loaded up their money and walked over to *Another Adventure*. Brody and I were left alone with a half million in cash. She was staring at me with a look that I could only describe as admiration.

"You are something else," she said. "And I love you for it."

"I love you too," I said. "But I'm just me, little old Breeze."

"We came here to make amends," she said. "And you end up walking away the hero. I can't comprehend how that worked out."

"I simply stumbled into an opportunity to help my friends," I said. "Dumb luck."

"But you seized it," she said. "You basically took over the whole operation and steered everyone else in the right direction. I wouldn't have known where to start. Plus I'd have been scared shitless of those dudes tonight."

"Who said I wasn't afraid?" I said.

"But you kept your wits about you somehow," she said.

"When events are out of control, stay calm," I said. "At least try not to piss your pants. Think. Take action when appropriate. Find an angle."

"I love how your mind works," she said. "You're a special man."

"Meanwhile, I'm thinking about what went wrong," I said. "That damn stuck prop, not checking the anchor light. It could have gone ugly somewhere along the line. I've lost a step I'm afraid."

"You were just out of practice," she said. "Next time you'll nail every little detail."

"Next time?"

"I've got a feeling this won't be our last adventure," she said. "Something tells me that these scenarios seek you out."

"Seems that way sometimes," I said. "We did manage a full year of peace and calm."

"And we both got a little bored," she said.

"I can handle any amount of boredom as long as you're around," I said. "But we'll be busy getting home soon."

"Let's stash this cash and hit the sack," she said.

"Deal."

We spent the next day loading groceries, topping off the fuel tanks, and taking on water. A quick glance at the charts showed less than five hundred miles to Grand Cayman. We decided to skip a stop in Mexico. We'd be on the open water for three days, but much closer to home. We met Tommy and Holly under the tiki for drinks and snacks. It was a bitter sweet occasion. Holly had cleaned up and tamed her wild hair somewhat. She couldn't stop smiling and she looked absolutely radiant. Brody had put on a pretty little sundress and even a touch of makeup. She was more gorgeous with each passing day. I was clean-shaven for a change. I stood there contemplating my past and my future. They were both embodied by the women who stood before me. Holly would sail away on another adventure. Brody and I would take a leap of faith back to America.

Our little cocktail party was winding down when Holly pulled me aside. I looked back at Brody, but she nodded that it was okay. We walked to a dark spot next to the mangroves.

"We both suck at goodbyes," I said.

"Listen, Breeze," she said. "You'll always be special to me, but Brody can love you like I can't. Just promise me that you'll do the same for her. All the way this time."

"I promise," I said. "And thank you, Holly. Thanks for everything."

"Thanks goes to you, captain," she said. "I feel like I've really matured because of you. I'm ready for the next step in life. There's a whole big world out there, and I'm going to see it all."

"Good luck to you."

"Good luck, Breeze."

I took her hand in mine. She pulled me in and kissed me on the lips for a long time.

"One for the road," she said.

Brody and Tommy were cleaning up when we returned. The party was over. We all said our goodbyes and went back to our boats. Back onboard, Brody didn't ask about my conversation with Holly. Instead, she took me to bed and helped me to forget all about her. It was a fitting end to that chapter in my life. *Godspeed Holly.*

I found a corroded wire connection running to the anchor light in the morning. That was the last issue that needed to be addressed. We shoved off and pointed the bow towards Grand Cayman. The sea was gently rolling under a cloudless sky. *Miss Leap's* engine purred like a contented kitten. She was happy to be heading back to Florida, as were we. All systems were go and a course was laid in towards a new future.

Brody stayed with me on the bridge all day. We talked while the autopilot did its thing.

"Seems like you've been sleeping better," she said.

"I haven't had a bad dream since we first met up with Holly and Tommy in Guatemala," I said.

"Excellent," she said. "A well-rested Breeze is a happy Breeze."

"I can't imagine being happier," I said.

"Me neither," she said. "Brody and Breeze in a world all their own."

The engine droned on as our bow sliced the small waves effortlessly. We saw no other vessels. We barely saw any clouds, just an ocean of blue. It was as if we were the only two living souls on the planet. Things couldn't have been going any better. We were sitting on a mountain of cash. The boat was performing flawlessly. We were closer to each other than we'd ever been. All was right with the world.

Brody went to bed soon after dark. I sat at the helm, looking at the stars. In spite of all of my screw-ups, I'd somehow made it to the top of the world. What was once a dream was now a reality. I'd been an embezzler, drug dealer, smuggler, tax evader, and all around miscreant. I'd been poorer than dirt with no hope, but that was behind me. I was feeling pretty self-satisfied until I thought about Bobby Beard.

Somehow, Brody's comment about how well I was sleeping made me think of him. Soon, he was all I could think about. If someone tells you not to think about pink elephants, you won't be able to think about anything else for a while. When my shift came to an end, I didn't want to go to bed. Brody insisted so I left the helm and made my way to our bunk. It smelled like her. The pleasant Brody aroma helped me fall asleep. Life was good, I told myself. Think about that.

It didn't work. He came to me later. Bobby Beard memories in vivid detail took over my dreams. I saw him with Jennifer at the Upper Deck, drinking beer and smiling. I saw him towing One-legged Beth on their way to Fort Myers. I saw him fighting a street thug in Rio Dulce. Finally, I saw him taunting me, challenging me to fight. I woke up before I could see myself beating him to a pulp.

I was alone in a dark bunk, somewhere in the middle of the ocean. I was no longer on top of the world. I was heavy with guilt. I'd survived, but Bobby had not. I'd been handed love and wealth while his corpse rotted in the ground. I didn't deserve to have it so good. None of the bad things I'd done in my life could compare to killing Bobby Beard. It wasn't something I could fix or even properly apologize for. It was final. At that moment, I felt like I'd live with him in my dreams for the rest of my life. I could have Brody when I was awake, but Bobby ruled my sleep.

I started the coffee maker and climbed up to the bridge. Brody was reading from her tablet.

"You're up early," she said.

"Bad dream," I said.

"Oh no," she said. "I thought we were past that."

"Apparently not," I said. "My mind was on gold, pirates, Valdez and Hector. Bobby never entered my thoughts, until now."

"When we get back we need to get you some help," she said.

"Like what? A shrink?"

"I'll look into it as soon as we get Wi-Fi," she said. "Try not to think about it."

A light breeze had picked up. Thin clouds were scattered amongst the stars. We were making great time, chugging along at seven knots. The salt air cleared my head. Brody brought up two cups of coffee and stayed with me. I was grateful. We could both catnap throughout the day. We watched the sunrise together there on the bridge. Everything was good again until I heard the engine miss a beat. I scanned all the gauges but found nothing awry. The engine sputtered again.

I scrambled down the ladder and grabbed a flashlight. I opened the hatch to the bilge and crawled to the fuel filters. I had two Racors but only ran off one at a time. I could see water in the bowl of the one I was using. I switched over to the good filter and listened to the engine. It soon smoothed out. I went back up and told Brody that we'd gotten bad fuel in Belize, before draining the water and changing the filter. I had three more spares after that one. I hoped that would be enough to get us into the marina in George Town, Grand Cayman. If not, we'd float helplessly in the open ocean. I tried to do the math in my head. We'd run for twenty hours before the filter was clogged. We needed to run another forty-seven or so hours to get there. That would be two, maybe three more filters. We'd be cutting it close.

I fought the fuel system during the day and I fought with Bobby Beard at night. The seas picked up and we slowed down. Eight hours out of port, I used the last of the filters. The seas got worse, further stirring up our remaining fuel. We were only fifteen miles out when the engine quit again.

"What do we do now?" asked Brody.

"I'll think of something," I said.

I crawled back into the bilge. The filter bowl was full of water, which I drained. I pulled the filter out and took it up on deck. It didn't look that dirty. I surmised that water was the main issue. I reinstalled it, and the engine fired. I brought Brody down in the bilge to show her what was going on. I made her lay down there while I drove, with instruction to drain the water before the bowl was full. She didn't like it much, but she did it. We managed to limp the rest of the way and get safely docked before the engine quit again. Brody was drenched in sweat as she climbed up out of the bilge.

"We don't move again until that problem is fixed," she said. "It had to be a hundred and fifty degrees down there."

"We'll take care of it," I assured her. "Cruising is all about fixing things in exotic places."

We used the showers at the yacht club and ate a nice meal. We had another three-day leg over big water to reach Florida. Solving our fuel issue was a top priority. We couldn't risk the crossing unless we were certain the problem was resolved completely. We were both worn out from the past three days of nonstop travel. We turned in early. Bobby Beard left me alone for a change. I slept well and woke with renewed energy and enthusiasm.

After breakfast, I started asking around for help with contaminated fuel. I was told to see Theo.

"Theo the cab driver?" I asked. "I know him."

"He got cabs still. He got a whole shop now. Does most anything. If he can't help he'll know someone who can."

We got a lift to Theo's, Grand Cayman's most eclectic new business enterprise. When Theo recognized me, he showed all of his white teeth in a great big smile.

"Welcome to Theo's," he said. "You like it?"

"What is it?"

"Cab service, limo service, exterminator, shipping broker, office supplies and passport photos," he said. "You need it I got it."

"Wow, man," I said. "You've come a long way. Congratulations."

"What brings you back here?" he asked. "And who's the pretty lady?"

I made the introductions and explained that we were on our way back to Florida after a year in the Caribbean.

"Must be the life," he said. "Lovely ladies on blue water."

"It's great until your boat breaks down," I told him.

"What is the problem?" he asked.

"Bad fuel," I said. "It's got a bunch of water in it."

"I got an oil transfer pump," he said. "I'll send a man to pump it out into drums and haul it off."

"You really can do it all," I said. "How's the wife?"

"She is wonderful," he said. "She stays home and takes care of the children."

"You had another kid?"

"Yes sir," he said. "Pretty as the first one."

"Sounds like you're doing fine my friend."

"Life is good," he said. "We are happy."

"Excellent news."

Theo arranged for the bad fuel to be removed. I bought a special funnel to pour new fuel through in case it too was contaminated. When I tried to find new fuel filters, they were not available. I'd have to have them shipped in. I went back to Theo for assistance.

"Do you have your temporary cruising permit?" he asked.

"Nope."

"Passport?"

"Yes."

"I will make it work," he said. "I got copies of other permits."

"I need 2040 Racors," I said. "Get me a dozen of them."

"Gonna take a few days," he said. "Enjoy your stay."

I was able to buy oil and a new oil filter at the yacht club store. I spent a day taking care of all the regular maintenance that had been neglected. Brody spent her day walking the city streets. George Town is a modern city, clean and safe. We hadn't seen anything like it since we left Florida. The next day we went to lunch at Tiki Beach. We sipped champagne cocktails on the ocean front patio until it got too hot. We retreated to the shade for conch fritters and fish sandwiches. The following night, Theo drove us to the Calypso Grill for dinner. It was a Caribbean-French combination. The tuna was excellent. It was nice to experience true civilization for a change. The people were universally friendly, and Theo was a courteous host.

Finally, the new fuel filters arrived and we were almost ready to depart. Brody got us a few more groceries, and a case of Caybrew, known as the Beer of the Cayman Islands. Both of us were itching to move on. I said goodbye to Theo and thanked him for his help. It was likely that I'd never see him again. We took *Leap of Faith* for a two-hour joy ride just to make sure everything was in order. We shoved off for good at first light the next morning.

The weather forecast was good, except for the ever-present threat of afternoon thunderstorms. I put us on a course that would take us well west of Cuban waters and engaged the autopilot. We cruised along without incident all day and into the night. When I finally went to sleep, Bobby Beard decided to haunt me once again. He taunted me, challenging me to fight. He called me an old man. He said he was taking over, Holly and all. I woke up and moved to the settee, but he followed me there in my dreams. This time he was in a hospital bed, clinging to life. It was another fight that he would eventually lose.

All of the guilt came rushing back. I sat up in the salon and listened to the drone of *Miss Leap's* engine. Brody was at the helm and in control. I wondered how she controlled her own guilt. She didn't seem to be affected by having shot a man. If she was, she hid it well. I decided to ask her about it.

"It takes time," she said. "Memories fade. I still think about it sometimes, but I don't let it eat me up."

"I still think about my wife too," I said. "But you're right. It hurts less now."

"You're going to be fine," she said. "We are going to be fine."

"Florida here we come," I said.

The next two nights were much the same. I battled Bobby and slept very little. I considered chugging some rum before bed, but I had a rule against drinking while we were underway. It was a good rule, so I stuck to it. We neared the lower Keys and watched a line of storms move from east to west. I turned east to steer clear of them. I decided to make landfall at Boot Key Harbor, in Marathon. It added fifty miles to the trip but another seven hours wouldn't kill us. We dropped the hook outside the harbor just after dark.

I'd spent quite a bit of time in Boot Key Harbor. I'd met some good folks and some bad ones. It was a good spot to stop for a day or two, get some rest and take a decent shower. Now that we were no longer underway, I cracked open a new bottle of rum. I got comfortably numb before Brody took me to bed and humped my brains out. I slept deeply with no bad dreams. I reported that to Brody in the morning.

"Rum and sex equal a good night's sleep," I said. "I really needed it."

"Just don't drink so much that you miss the sex part," she said.

"Good advice."

We entered the harbor and picked up a mooring ball. Our first stop was the shower house. Our second stop was Keys Fisheries for raw oysters and cold beer. Brody was disappointed that stone crabs were out of season, but she was thrilled to be back in Florida.

"Just feels good to be in America," she said. "You know what I mean?"

"I feel it too," I said. "It'll be good to get back to Pelican Bay."

"Not before hanging out somewhere with people, and fast food, and real stores," she said. "Solitude can wait a little while."

"We'll stop in Fort Myers Beach," I said. "See how the gang is doing. Maybe run up to Fort Myers to see how Beth is making out."

"Can we get a marina slip at some point?" she asked. "Maybe run the air conditioner?"

"Can't let you get too soft," I said.

"I'm still a woman," she said. "I could use a little pampering."

"You know, you're right," I admitted. "You've been a fantastic sport for a year now, a real trooper. We can afford it for a while."

"Someplace with a pool," she suggested.

"I'll see what I can do."

Nine

We tried the rum and sex trick again, but it didn't work. I didn't tell Brody because I liked the rum and the sex. We were ready to head north. Each trip was a single day. We could anchor every night, drink, and make love.

It took three days to make it to Fort Myers Beach. Bobby had shown up each of those three nights. Finally, I had to break down and admit it to Brody.

"We're in the land of free Wi-Fi," she said. "There's a book I want you to read. I'll download it for you."

I took her to the Lighthouse Resort where they had excellent Wi-Fi and Taco Tuesday. They also had a pool, which we crashed after lunch. Brody downloaded the book and handed her tablet to me.

The book was called *On Killing: The Psychological Cost of Learning to Kill in War and Society*. It was written by Dave Grossman, a retired lieutenant colonel in the United States Army.

"It was required reading at the FBI Academy," said Brody.

"What's the gist?" I asked.

"I don't want to influence your perception of it," she said. "Read it for yourself."

After getting her to show me how to use the device, I started to read Grossman's book. I was almost immediately skeptical. It is his contention that men are loathe to kill and simply won't do it. The military overcomes this natural aversion to killing through training and conditioning. In other words, it takes innocent pacifists and turns them into killing machines. The problem comes when these newly minted killers are returned to civil society. I got that last part but wholly disagreed with the first part.

Men have been freely killing other men since Cain killed Abel. We have thousands of years of evidence of man's willingness to kill. People kill each other all the time, women included. Grossman based his claims on the work of one Samuel Lyman Atwood Marshall, or SLAM. He claimed to have done thousands of interviews with combat veterans. He also claimed that as many as eighty percent of them never fired their weapon, or purposely missed, due to their aversion to killing another human being. I found that to be an extraordinary claim. I asked Brody what she thought.

"Google it," she said.

I did a quick search for this SLA Marshall fellow. The way Google sees it, his research was basically bullshit. It's been debunked over and over again, with all attempts to replicate his findings resulting in failure. The author of the book I was reading was using his bogus statistics to back up his entire thesis.

It was a tough slog, but I kept on reading. Grossman had a way of using his personal anecdotal evidence and making it sound like legitimate research. I kept referring back to Google to verify some of his claims. Not all of them were dubious, but some of them were. I began to doubt that he'd ever seen actual combat. Turns out he hadn't. How do you call yourself an expert on killing in war when you've never been to war? The book did cause me to feel sympathetic to those who've actually survived combat. I don't think society has handled them very well, especially post-Vietnam. We seem to show a little more respect these days, but I'd still seen plenty of homeless vets in my travels. It was clear that their experience had changed them. I'd never asked any of them about killing though. I found myself wanting to talk to someone who had actually killed in combat. I'd like to see what they'd say about Grossman's theories.

About three quarters through the book, the author switched up topics. He started talking about violent video games and violence in media. He claimed that violent crime was up in correspondence with the increased use of video games. I had to look that up too. This internet thing was indeed useful. Current statistics disproved his claim. Violent crimes were actually somewhat reduced over the past ten years. I thought about the murder rates and the amount of violence in countries that didn't even have video games. I wondered about all of the death and destruction the world had seen since the beginning of time, and how it had nothing to do with modern media or a new culture of violence among our youth.

"They made you read this at Quantico?" I asked Brody.

"It was required," she said. "Many police forces are also required to read it."

"Doesn't say much about civilian shootings," I said.

"Cops don't consider themselves civilians," she said.

"I suppose not," I said. "This guy seems smart. I appreciate the fact that he seems to care about our soldiers, but there are big holes in theories that he advances. Plus it doesn't help me personally at all. Other than the shared regret of having killed."

"I'd think you're going to have to find a way to forgive yourself," she said.

"Let me ask you this," I said. "What if it had happened in America, say in a bar or something?"

"At the street level, no one would think you were guilty of a crime."

"But what about in a court of law?" I asked.

"Any decent prosecutor would push for manslaughter charges," she said. "No premeditation, or as they say, malice aforethought. You had no prior intention of killing him."

"What about self-defense?"

"We still have the use of deadly force," she explained. "Even if it was your honest opinion that it was justified."

"What kind of sentence does it carry?"

"Varies by state," she said. "Florida has a mandatory minimum sentence of nine years, I think."

"I wonder what the law in Guatemala says."

"I imagine the sentence is harsh," she said. "But a conviction would be tricky given the circumstances. No reliable witness and a deathbed confession. You'd most likely walk."

"So I'm left to judge myself," I said. "Therein lies the problem."

"I think it's good that you're torn up about it," she said. "I'd be worried if it didn't bother you at all."

"I don't want it to hinder our relationship," I told her.

"We're in this together," she said. "We'll work it out."

She'd had her own experience with taking a life. I started to wonder more about that, and her future career. Since we were being open with one another, I asked her about it.

"What's going to happen with you and the FBI?" I asked.

"I can't go back now," she said. "They did a nice job of sweeping my shooting under the rug. A street cop would have been crucified in the court of public opinion and probably lost their job. I got paid for a while, with all the support I could ask for, but the hiatus wasn't my idea."

"They asked you to disappear for a while?"

"Something like that," she said. "Told me to take all the time I needed."

"Would they take you back?"

"Legally, they'd have to," she said. "But I got the distinct impression that they'd rather I not return."

"Indefinite unpaid leave," I said.

"A career killer," she said. "I'd never get anywhere in the Bureau. I'd get all the shitty assignments, new partners constantly. I'd be mopping toilets in Siberia."

"I guess you'll just have to keep on living a life of luxury aboard our fine vessel," I said.

"I definitely traded up," she said. "Thanks, Breeze."

"It's your fault," I said. "You found me."

I was finished talking about the book, and the FBI. I wasn't good at real world problems. I could fix most things in my own little world. We decided to get cleaned up and go listen to some live music. We'd have a few drinks and forget about the troubles of the day. It was Monday night, and that meant Scott Bryan was playing at the Upper Deck. It also meant seeing Jennifer, if she was still tending the bar.

She was absolutely shocked when she saw me and Brody walk in, but she recovered quickly.

"I was pretty sure I'd never see you again," she said. "You both look great."

"Old habits die hard," I said. "Good to see you."

"You remember Jason," she said, pointing to her boyfriend.

The last time I'd met him, she had warned me not to mess things up for them. I had no reason to interfere. The last time I'd meddled in her relationship, it had led to the whole Bobby Beard debacle.

"You remember Brody," I said.

"FBI right?" she said.

"I was," said Brody. "But I've accepted the position of first mate aboard Breeze's boat."

"Good for you," said Jennifer. "Maybe you can keep him straight."

It was a friendly and easy exchange. Brody had a way to make people feel comfortable. She'd staked her claim without pissing anyone off. We ordered our drinks and moved to a high-top to listen to the music. Scotty was playing all the songs we loved and doing a good job of it. It felt good to be on familiar turf.

"So what's next?" asked Brody.

"I'd like to hang out a few days," I said. "Catch up with the gang. See if there's any word on Beth."

"The boat is a mess," she said. "It needs a good scrubbing. We're going to need lots of water."

"I can jug it from here," I said. "But it would be much easier if we were in a marina."

"What's here, as far as marinas?"

"Expensive and snobby," I said. "I know a place north of here. The scrubbing can wait."

"You're the captain," she said.

We caught up with Robin the very next day. He was on his way to dive a boat in the harbor but stopped by when he saw *Leap of Faith*.

He hadn't heard from Beth. He'd moved his boat to a slip and was working as the dock master at Island Bay Marina. Diver Dan came by later in the afternoon. He hadn't heard from Beth either. He had a new girlfriend. He'd been spending time on her boat fishing and exploring. Life was good.

I learned that my old friend Jamie Brown had passed away from cancer. His boat, *Bay Dreamer*, had been sold and was no longer in the harbor. It gave me pause. He was only a few years older than me. He'd been super friendly whenever we got together. He had spent a lot of time in Pelican Bay. I knew he'd been battling brain cancer, but I thought he'd beat it. Another good one had gone too soon. I'd done a good job of living a life on my own terms, but it was a stark reminder to enjoy every day. I gave Brody a big hug and asked her to make love to me. I couldn't think of a better way to celebrate life.

We ran out of things to do in Fort Myers Beach, so we decided to cruise up the Caloosahatchee River and check on Beth. I found her sailboat, but she wasn't on it. A young couple was. They'd bought the boat from Beth. I asked what happened to her.

"She's got that Carver powerboat over there," the girl told me. "Moved up in the world."

One-legged Beth wasn't aboard, so we dropped anchor nearby and waited. She came out in her skiff in the early evening. She saw my boat and came straight over. She'd cut her hair short and gained a few more pounds. Her eyes were clear and bright.

"Tie off and climb aboard," I said.

When she climbed over the rail I noticed her new prosthetic. She really had moved up in the world. We hugged and laughed.

"Looks like you're doing well here," I said.

"I am doing just fine, thank you," she said. "Never better. What are you doing here?"

"I came to see you," I said. "No one has heard from you so I guess I was a little worried."

"No need to worry," she said. "It's all good. I figured if I was starting a new life, I had to leave those guys behind. All of them."

"I'm glad to hear that you're doing well," I said. "Seriously."

"I owe it all to you," she said. "I try not to think about those days, but you saved my life."

"That's what friends are for," I said.

She stayed for an hour and drank a few beers, before heading back to her new boat. I was happy for her, and I could rest easy about her future. She was on the right track.

"That's another person whose life you changed," said Brody. "Theo told me about the money you gave him a few years back. He said it was what made him get his act together."

"I never gave Beth a dime and she's never asked," I said. "But I had to get her away from the drugs. Looks like she's making it on her own now."

"You're a good man, Meade Breeze," she said. "Give yourself some credit."

"I still need to even up the ledger," I said. "What little good I've done doesn't make up for all of the bad."

"I don't know about any ledger," she said. "But I don't think it works that way. Once you start doing good, you can be forgiven. I bet you've helped plenty of people along the way. Think about it."

I thought about the Cuban girl I had smuggled into the States and how I'd saved her from certain rape. I considered the fact that I'd had at least a small impact on political corruption in southwest Florida. I'd taken down a dirty lawyer and helped a clean water activist get elected. I'd rescued two sex slaves from the Russian Mafia. I'd helped old Shirley fulfill her dying wish. I had never once listed out the good deeds. I'd been focused on all the ways I'd gone wrong. Maybe I wasn't a lost cause after all.

"Thanks, Brody," I said. "That was helpful."

"Anytime, sailor," she said. "Now what do you want to do next?"

"I'd love for us to sit in Pelican Bay for a little while," I said. "I'll get you to a marina soon, but I want to go home first."

"Home," she said. "A novel concept."

"It's as much of a home as I have," I told her.

"It's lovely," she said. "If it had a grocery store I could stay there forever."

"Maybe we could get a little skiff," I suggested. "Use it to run to town for supplies."

"Marina first," she said. "You promised."

Ten

We left the next day for Pelican Bay. One-legged Beth, Diver Dan, and Robin were all doing well. Jennifer was happy with her man. Scott Bryan still sang songs every Monday night at the bar. Everyone was just fine without me hanging around. Other than Brody, there was no one depending on me for anything. I could relax and enjoy my time with her. We were happy about how things were working out for us.

Miss Leap was happy too. I could hear it in her hum and feel it at the helm. These were her home waters as much as they were mine. I was lucky to have her, as much as I was lucky to have Brody.

We anchored towards the southern end of the bay, just past Manatee Cove. We got settled in and fixed a fine dinner. We sat in silence as the sun went down. Everything was perfect until I went to sleep. The dreams were as vivid as ever. I watched a high-definition, surround sound movie featuring Bobby Beard being pummeled by a madman. I thought it would never end, but Brody shook me awake.

"Rum and sex?" she asked.

"Excellent idea," I answered.

I sipped straight rum on ice until things got a little fuzzy. I didn't stay awake long enough for the sex. When I woke up, I was on the settee alone. Brody was asleep in the bunk. I went outside and watched the sun come up. With it came the promise of a new day. I dismissed Bobby and vowed to enjoy every minute of it. That was accomplished by sitting in the water and drinking beer for hours.

Late in the afternoon, an old sailboat approached the entrance to Pelican Bay. We were on the beach watching. It started to go down the middle, which is the wrong thing to do, but quickly figured out where the channel was. He paralleled the narrow strip of sand that we were sitting on. I saw a thatch of pure white hair and a white mustache on the captain. He had to be in his eighties. The boat looked as old as him. We watched him slowly cross the bay until he was near *Leap of Faith*. He dropped anchor a hundred yards from our port side. It was a respectful distance, but I was usually alone down there. I didn't like company much.

He put his dinghy in the water. It was a little rowing dink. It always amazed me when an old geezer chose to row instead of using a motor. It reminded me of my old friend Shirley, who used to row to the ranger station every day for a Klondike Bar. He rowed over to *Miss Leap*, which I found curious. I didn't know him and he didn't know me. He floated there for a minute before returning to his boat.

"What was that all about?" asked Brody.

"I don't know," I said. "Think we should go find out?"

"Nothing else to do," she said. "Let's go talk to the old dude. He's probably got some stories to tell."

We hopped in our dinghy and motored over to check him out. He saw us coming and greeted us at the stern of his boat.

"We're on that trawler over there," I said. "Saw you go over there."

"You Breeze?" he asked.

"Depends on who's asking," I told him.

"My name's Cecil," he said. "Cecil Rogers."

"Want to tell me why you were snooping around my vessel, Cecil?"

"I'm looking for a fellow named Breeze," he said. "He's on *Leap of Faith*."

He looked harmless. He obviously knew my name and my boat's name. I couldn't imagine how he'd do us any harm.

"I'm Breeze," I said. "This is Brody."

"Pleased to meet you," he said.

"Why are you looking for me?" I asked. "How do you know who I am?"

"Long story," he said. "You're welcome to come aboard and listen to an old man for a spell."

We climbed aboard and took seats in the cockpit. The boat was old but it was in sound shape, kind of like its owner. Cecil seemed fit enough. His white hair was receding on his forehead. He sported eighty years' worth of wrinkles, but his eyes were sharp.

"What brings you here, old-timer?" I asked.

"Let me start at the beginning," he said. "Well, not the real beginning, but the beginning of this escapade."

"This ought to be good," I said. "Start with telling me how you know my name."

"I was in the Keys trying to sell a load of dope," he said.

"Wait, what?" said Brody.

"What's that got to do with me?" I asked.

"I'm getting to it," he said. "I was accosted by some goons and taken to a fellow named Bald Mark."

"I'm surprised you survived that encounter," I said.

"Took pity on me because I'm so old," he said. "I might have played up that fact a bit. He wouldn't allow me to sell my load anywhere down there. He said he couldn't make an exception for me because it would set a precedent. He told me you might be able to help."

"I'm long out of the dope business," I said.

"He said I might find you in Fort Myers Beach or here in this bay," he said.

"I've got no contacts up here," I told him. "I'm afraid I can't help you."

"I've got a thousand pounds of weed on board," he said. "I put everything I had into this deal. Stand to make a nice profit if I can get a decent price for it. I can't go home broke."

"What's this really all about, Cecil?" I asked. "How old are you anyway?"

"I'm eighty-three years old," he said. "I used to do this for a living. It's been a long time now though. I thought I could pull it off once more, for old-time's sake."

"You ran weed for a living?" asked Brody.

"Back in the day," he said. "By the ton sometimes. I smuggled it in from Jamaica at first. Later we made some connections in the Bahamas. Left Florida and set up a new operation in California. Anybody knows smuggling it's me."

"Except for the part about having a buyer lined up," I said.

"I had a guy in Miami," he said. "But he got busted while I was gone."

"And you ran afoul of the biggest drug kingpin in south Florida," I said.

"I'm out of touch, I guess," he said. "It ain't the seventies no more."

"I'm out of touch too," I told him. "I really don't know anyone who can handle that kind of quantity."

"My wife is long dead," he said. "Fool thing to do at my age. That weed is all I have left, besides this old boat."

He waved for me to go below. We went forward until I saw a big lump covered with a tarp. Cecil pulled the tarp off and revealed dozens of tightly sealed bales of pot.

"Fine Jamaican ganga," he said.

"You went all the way to Jamaica in this old boat?" asked Brody.

"Not that big of a deal," he said. "I've been on boats, captained boats, and owned boats all of my life. I've run power and I've run sail. Hell, had a small fleet of go-fast boats at one time. Kept the mother ship over in the Bahamas and offloaded to the smaller boats for transport to Miami."

We went back to the cockpit where Cecil put his head in his hands. I thought he might cry.

"You were my last hope in the world," he said. "I'm lost up this way. I don't know anyone or anywhere that I can sell my load. I fucked up right and royal this time."

"How'd you line up buyers back in the day?"

"When we first got started, we'd find the guy who sold ten pounds or so," he said. "Then we'd find the guy that he was buying from. Worked up the chain until we had the head honcho. Eventually, we didn't need to do that kind of leg work anymore. They came to us."

"Let me think about it," I said. "Maybe I can find the ten-pound guy, work it from there."

"You know someone that sells dope?" Brody asked.

"Remember, I used to sell dope," I said. "There's a guy not far from here that I could count on to take a few ounces at a time."

"A few ounces is a far cry from ten pounds, or a thousand pounds," said Cecil.

"It's all I've got," I said. "Won't hurt to try."

"I guess not," he said. "Thanks."

We all shook hands and our little party broke up.

Brody was full of questions when we got back to our boat. Who is this guy? How are we going to get there? How do we get in touch with him? Are you sure you want to do this?

"I feel sorry for the old codger," I said. "I'll just poke around a little and see what happens."

"We're just sitting here minding our own business, and this falls into your lap," she said. "I swear, Breeze. You're like some kind of drama magnet."

"Welcome to my world," I said. "This is pretty much how it always happens."

"I'll play along," she said. "But this is the perfect excuse to go to a marina."

"Fair enough," I said. "We'll leave tomorrow."

"Sweet," she said. "I'm so looking forward to it."

"Marinas can come with their own drama," I said. "Some of them are like trailer parks."

"I don't care," she said. "Just give me a long hot shower and unlimited electricity. Do you think we could rig up some air conditioning?"

"Slow down there missy," I said. "One step at a time. We're going to need to rent or buy a car for this job, and the grocery store is too far to walk to."

"A car?" she said. "Will wonders never cease."

"I know where this guy lives, but I don't have his phone number," I said.

"Says the guy who doesn't even own a phone," she said. "Of course you don't have his number."

"We'll just go pay him a visit," I said. "We'll tell Cecil our plans first. Maybe he'll want to come with us."

We went to talk to Cecil before leaving. He said he couldn't afford to stay in a marina. I told him about an anchorage about a mile south of where we were going. He could hole up near Don Pedro Island while we tried to hunt down a buyer. Both boats left Pelican Bay and headed north. I took us to Palm Island Marina in Cape Haze, where I'd stayed previously. It was a quiet little place well off the beaten path. I was barely tied up to the dock when Brody took off for the shower house. I was sporting a less than pleasant aroma myself. There was no point in staying dirty if Brody was clean. There is nothing like a good shower after many days at sea. Any liveaboard cruiser will tell you that.

We thought about how nice it would be to have sex since we were both nice and clean, but we decided to just enjoy not being dirty for a little longer. Brody wanted to wash the sheets now that we had access to a laundry room. We'd been in the marina for an hour and I was already feeling domesticated. I started figuring out how to install an air conditioner. Brody discovered the free Wi-Fi. We met our neighbors. We took a walk around the property and decided to have dinner at the on-sight restaurant. The service and the food were excellent.

"I could get used to this," said Brody. "Thanks so much for bringing me here."

"We can afford it," I said. "A little pampering won't hurt, but don't forget we've got a job to do."

"Did you ever smoke weed?" she asked.

"Once, with Holly," I said. "It was pleasant enough, but it blurred my senses. Definitely a hindrance to situational awareness."

"It made me paranoid," she said. "I didn't really like it."

"I don't have a moral problem with it," I said. "It's just not my cup of tea."

"Me neither," she said. "But it was a big no-no at the Bureau."

We lingered over after-dinner drinks and a shared dessert. We walked out to the pool to watch the sun go down. Other marina residents welcomed us. Someone blew a conch horn. I thought that maybe marina life wouldn't be so bad. Brody agreed.

The next day we shopped Craigslist for a car. Brody handled the phone calls and negotiations. Our neighbors gave us a ride into town where we purchased a clean little car for five grand. We loaded it with groceries after taking a spin around the neighborhood. Englewood was a nice town. We weren't too far from Venice either. Boca Grande was just to the south of us. Punta Gorda was thirty minutes away. We decided we liked the place.

Later that same day I bought a small window unit air conditioner and put it in the side door, near the lower helm. I measured the resulting open space and went to Home Depot to have a piece of plywood cut. It fit in the hole nicely. I fired it up and Brody squealed with delight. It made me happy to see her happy. We lazed the rest of the day away at the pool.

We took the dinghy out to pick up Cecil and treated him to dinner. I informed him that we planned to go find the first link in the pot supply chain the next day. He hinted at me buying his load from him and selling it myself.

"No way in hell," I said. "This isn't my gig. I'm just trying to find someone you can work with. The rest is up to you."

"As you can imagine, I'm beginning to regret this whole stupid idea," he said. "If I wasn't so broke, I'd dump the shit offshore. Be done with it."

"That would make the locals happy," I said. "When it started washing up on shore."

"Wouldn't be the first time," he said.

"It's funny," I said. "I've traveled thousands of miles out there, and I've yet to find any sort of drugs. I've walked hundreds of beaches, many of them remote, and still no glory. No square grouper, no bricks of coke, nothing."

"What would you do if you found something?" asked Brody.

"Damn good question," I admitted. "Especially if it was cocaine. I wouldn't know what to do with, or how to get rid of it."

"Or if it had a GPS tracker in it," she said. "More likely than not these days."

"Good point," I said. "Probably just leave it be then. Let it float."

"Stuff floated up on beaches all the time back in the seventies," said Cecil. "Occupational hazard. Sometimes it had to be tossed. I broke down once in one of the fast boats. I was a sitting duck, and fully prepared to dump my load. Boss man sent another boat from Miami and with repair parts."

"Sounds like things were pretty wild back then," I said.

"There were so many boats running back and forth you couldn't count them," he said. "The Coast Guard was overwhelmed and didn't make smoking dope a high priority. It's when the coke started coming in that things changed. Dope smugglers didn't usually carry guns. If you lost a bale or two, no one was going to kill you for it. Damn Columbians would cut your throat if you snorted a gram of their product. Ruined it for everyone."

"Is that why you went to California?" I asked.

"I don't recall the timing all that well," he said. "But we'd gotten too big to keep running the operation the same way. Sooner or later we'd get popped."

"You never got caught?" asked Brody.

"Not directly," he said. "Did some jail time, though. I made so much money out there I didn't know what to do with it. I couldn't spend it all or figure out what to buy next. I got out. My wife and I went home to Georgia. I thought it was all over. Years later, somehow it all came back to bite me in the ass. I did a few years easy time."

"After that?"

"We set up a little boutique bakery," he said. "I'd had some success in retail with a marine hardware business in Fort Lauderdale. She died in 2008."

"And after all this time, you got the itch to be a smuggler again?" I asked. "Nothing to lose?"

"I told you, I regret the choice now," he said. "Seemed like an adventure when I cooked up the idea."

"Give me some time," I said. "Maybe it will work out after all."

"Don't see where I have any other choice," he said.

We took him back to his boat and said good night. His grand plan to go out in style did indeed seem like a fool idea, but I was even more determined to help the old guy. We got up early the next day and went to find the man named Art. When we arrived, we saw a car in the driveway. I went to the front door and knocked.

"Holy crap, Breeze," he said. "What's it been? Five years?"

"It's been a while," I said.

"Let me tell you right up front," he said. "I've got a steady supplier now. I don't need to buy your homegrown."

"I don't have any homegrown to sell," I said. "I've got good Jamaican, but most likely in a quantity you can't handle."

"I've been getting a pound or two at a time," he said.

"So the guy you've been getting it from, he's probably holding a lot more than that."

"He told me he can get as much as ten pounds," he said.

"Can you hook me up with him?" I asked.

"You've got ten pounds?"

"It's a lot more than that," I said. "And it's not really mine. I'm trying to broker a deal for a much larger quantity."

"I doubt this guy can handle it," he said.

"That's why I need to meet the guy he buys from," I explained. "Maybe even the next guy up the line."

"All I know is my guy gets his from the east coast," he said. "I get along with him pretty well. I'll ask him discreetly."

"That's all I can ask," I said. "Good to see you again, Art. How's it been going?"

That was a mistake. I got to hear about his cancer scare. He told me that his girlfriend was moving out. He bemoaned the fact that he'd soon be seventy years old. What is with these old guys and pot? Eventually, Brody reminded me of an imaginary appointment. We needed to run. I gave him Brody's phone number and we left.

"Thanks, Brody," I said. "Good job getting me out of there."

"We're a team," she said. "Remember?"

There was nothing else to do but wait for Art to call. We went back to our little marina oasis and our trawler trash air conditioning. Bobby Beard decided to revisit me in my dreams that night. This time it pissed me off, not just because of what I'd done to him, but because I couldn't shake it. I was in complete control of my life, except for in my dreams. Life had never been better, but those dreams were a true fly in the ointment. I had to find a way to get past it. Brody suggested trying some of the organizations that help veterans with PTSD.

"I don't deserve to be tagged with PTSD," I told her. "I'm not a combat veteran. Those guys are heroes. I'm a boat bum."

"They've killed," she said. "They've seen a lot of death. Coping mechanisms may be similar."

"I'll give it some thought," I said.

Art called a few days later. His supplier had agreed to talk, but I needed to bring some product. I went out to Cecil's boat, took a picture of the whole pile, and dug out an ounce or so of weed. As soon as I broke the seal on the bale, the pungent odor of dope filled the boat. Cecil freaked out.

"If the marine patrol gets anywhere near me I'm screwed," he said.

"Seal it back up," I said. "You've got some duct tape don't you?"

"I should be in a rocking chair on my front porch in Georgia," he said.

"Yes you should," I said. "But I'm making progress. Can't quit now."

We drove to Arcadia to meet Art's supplier. His place was out in the sticks. We missed the drive the first time and had to backtrack to find it. It wasn't quite out of the script from Deliverance, but it was close. Brody was armed for the occasion. The guy was working on a four-wheel drive pickup truck when we reached the house. I expected some toothless redneck, but he turned out to be a clean-cut, well-groomed middle aged man.

"You're Art's friend, right?" he said.

"Breeze," I said. "This is Brody."

"Welcome to my ranch," he said. "We'll just keep this friendly and informal, okay?"

"How do we proceed?"

"You state your business so I'm not a victim of entrapment," he said. "Tell me you're not the law and such."

"We have no connection to law enforcement," I assured him. "We're trying to get rid of a thousand pounds of pot."

"Whoa," he said. "I don't have that kind of money."

"We're thinking maybe the guy you're buying from might," I explained.

"I don't know," he said. "That's a big slug of money all at once."

"I brought a sample," I said. "Show him the picture, Brody."

He inspected what I'd brought, and took a look at the photo. I could sense the wheels turning in his head. The dude was trying to figure out how to make money off this deal.

"If you know someone, or can find someone, that can afford to buy a thousand pounds, I'll pay you a finder's fee," I said.

"I might know someone," he said. "How much?"

"Ten grand," I offered.

"More like twenty," he countered.

"Fifteen."

"All right," he said. "I'm not certain, but I might be able to get it bought. I don't normally run in those circles. I'll ask around."

I'd been carefully studying him throughout our conversation. My instinct told me that he was on the up and up. Art was a good guy and he trusted him. Besides, I was a step removed. I wouldn't be the one out on the street advertising for a big buyer. He was willing to take the risk for fifteen grand. I looked to Brody for confirmation. She nodded in agreement.

"Keep the sample," I said. "Call this number when you've got something for us."

"Have you thought about crew and location if and when this deal goes down?" he asked.

"You don't need to know those particulars yet," I said. "Call when you are ready."

The truth was I hadn't thought that far ahead. I'm glad he put the idea in my head. I needed to find a secluded spot that Cecil could get his boat into, with land and road access.

Eleven

I looked over the charts for a nearby hidey hole. We were on the ICW just north of Boca Grande and just south of Englewood. There was a park on Lemon Bay that might have worked. We checked it out the next day. There were a bunch of people hanging out and several boats anchored just offshore. It was a no. There was a dock on Ski Alley on the inside of Stump Pass. Unfortunately, it had a gate that was locked at sunset. We couldn't get a truck to it. All of the deep water spots with easy road access were in well-populated areas or parks that were gated.

We took a dinghy ride down to where Cecil was anchored. Almost directly across the waterway was a small dock. It was part of Don Pedro State Park. I knew there was a gate at the entrance, but I'd never seen it closed. There were no rangers assigned to this section of the park. I tied up to the dock and stuck an oar down to check for depth. I didn't touch bottom with the four-foot long oar.

The dinghy had no depth finder, but I could see the bottom. I guessed it was five feet deep. We looked up the tide charts later and found that we'd checked the depth at the top of a high tide.

We went over and asked Cecil what his draft was. He said five feet.

"Is that an honest five feet?" I asked. "Or is it more like four and a half, or four-nine?"

"It's five," he said. "I've touched bottom enough to know."

Getting his boat to that little dock was going to be tricky. The exchange would have to take place at the top of the high tide, no matter what time that was. The gate would have to be open. It wasn't ideal. We drove by the gate after dark three times. It was always open. We kept looking at tide charts. The high was getting to be in the middle of the night, which was perfect, except we hadn't heard from our man yet. All we could do was wait.

The wait took its toll on Cecil. It was hot and the breeze had been non-existent. He was low on food and water. The uncertainty was nerve wracking. I got tired of listening to him whine, so I paid for him to have a slip for a few days. We helped him get tied up so he could fill his water tanks, take a shower, and cool off in the pool. We spent our evening sitting around the pool, drinking beer and telling stories. Cecil had a bunch of good tales to tell from his days as a smuggler, but the more he drank the more political he became.

It started with a conversation about marijuana. None of us were against it, but Cecil was an activist in favor of it. He was pissed at the state of Florida for what he saw as a rejection of the voter's wishes. It was true that Florida voters overwhelmingly approved of medical marijuana, but the legislature had allowed individual counties to ban dispensaries. So far the only products available for medical use were oils and edibles, and it didn't appear that smoking marijuana would ever be allowed, even for medicinal purposes. Cecil figured we should legalize it period, for both medical and recreational uses.

That didn't bother me too much. I wasn't sure about legal recreational use, but it didn't really concern me. We all thought that medical use should be available for those that needed it. My problem with Cecil came up when he expanded his political diatribes to include just about every left-wing, social justice warrior talking point. I very much believed in a live and let live philosophy. I'd met good people and bad people on both sides of the political aisle. I had little interest in either side's sermon. I wasn't well-versed in the latest political gossip because I didn't live in that world. I didn't watch television, didn't have the internet, and rarely listened to the radio. I was insulated from what was apparently a cold civil war going on in America between the left and the right.

Cecil made it clear that he felt strongly about his various causes. He also made it clear that he had little tolerance for those with a different opinion. For the most part, I had no opinion either way. Brody didn't have much to say either. We hadn't talked about politics specifically, but I'd gathered that if pushed, she'd identify as a conservative. Listening to Cecil rant, I was grateful for my disinterest. Finally, I'd had enough, so I told him so.

"Cool it with the politics, man," I said. "It's not in my top ten as far as interests go. I don't keep up with it."

"Ignorance is bliss I suppose," he said. "You may not be interested in politics, but politics is interested in you."

"That's my problem with it in a nutshell," I said. "I just want to be left alone. I don't need nor want anyone's government telling me what I can and cannot do."

"As beneficiaries of a free society, we all have an obligation to help those less fortunate," he said. "Don't you agree?"

"I'm helping you, old man," I said. "Don't you agree?"

"I mean on a bigger scale," he said. "It is our duty to help others. It is our duty to protect the Earth from global warming. It is our duty to provide education equally to all, as well as health care."

"When you were smuggling all that dope back in the seventies," I began. "Did you pay taxes on all of your earnings?"

"Of course not," he admitted. "The IRS would have found me out quite easily."

"So you denied the government money that was rightfully theirs?" I asked. "Money that could have gone to welfare, food stamps, student loans?"

"It's different," he said.

"How much of that money did you donate to worthy causes?" I asked. "You said you were loaded. Did you help out the local food bank?

Anonymously send money to the IRS for the betterment of all Americans?"

"I didn't think much of it at the time," he admitted.

"Sounds like your beliefs have changed over time," I said. "You were a capitalist, whether you want to admit it or not. You were also a tax evader, just like me. It was your money and you didn't want to share it with the government."

"I couldn't," he said. "It was illegally obtained."

"Say what you want, Cecil," I said. "You talk the progressive talk, but you haven't walked the progressive walk."

"You sound like you are against my admittedly liberal ideology," he said.

"I don't care what your ideology is," I said. "But if you're going to be a progressive, be a good one. Do your part to change the world. Pontificating at poolside accomplishes nothing."

"I was just carrying on a conversation," he said. "No offense intended."

"Let's call a truce, then," I said. "And change the subject."

Brody took the cue and chimed in. She asked what we were going to do if the call we were waiting for never came.

"I hope it doesn't come to that," I said. "I don't know. Maybe I could work something out with Bald Mark, but I'd rather not try."

"Too bad I can't donate weed to a worthy cause," said Cecil.

"Wait just a minute," I said. "What about those dispensaries we were talking about? Can we sell it to one of them?"

"Damn good question," he said. "Hadn't considered that angle."

"I think that dispensaries grow their own, or have a close relationship to a grower," said Brody. "They have certain standards that have to be maintained."

"I think it's worth some research," I said. "Do you mind looking into it?"

"Of course not," she said. "Google is your friend."

"I think that states where recreational pot is available would be a better bet than Florida," Cecil said. "I assume they have state approved growers, but there's always a possibility they buy from whomever they can."

"We're a long way from Colorado," I said.

"It's funny," he said. "If it was legalized, there would be no reason for people like me to smuggle it in. But here I am."

"Let's not forget that it is not legal," Brody said. "Especially in the quantity you have."

"I'd hate to go back to jail," he said.

"There's a risk," I said. "We don't know who we're dealing with. Might be cops."

"You think that guy would take your money and call the cops?" she asked.

"Maybe we're stepping on his territory," I said. "As small as it may be."

"He hasn't called yet," she said. "And we haven't paid him yet."

"Maybe we should just drop the whole thing," Cecil said. "I'll survive somehow."

"Don't dump it offshore," Brody said. "Find a grower who supplies a medical marijuana dispensary. Donate it."

"I'm tiring of this rapidly," he said. "I'm embarrassed at my incompetence. I just want to go home. If something doesn't go down soon, I'm giving up."

It would have been easy to agree with him. Brody and I didn't need the drama, but I'd signed on to help him. I wanted to see it through.

"A few more days," I said. "Let's give it the old college try."

"A few more days," he said.

Three days later, Cecil was at the end of his rope. He was preparing to leave the dock and start heading back to Georgia. I paid to top off his fuel tanks. Brody went and bought him some groceries. Then we got the call. Our man had found a buyer, but only for half the load. There was no one in his circle or anyone in his circle that knew anyone, that could handle a thousand pounds. Half was better than nothing I supposed. The buyer wanted to send someone to lay eyes on the product, to verify it existed. They also wanted to identify the exchange location. I told them to be prepared to negotiate a price. I'd leave that to Cecil on our end. It was his dope.

"I'll still make a small profit," Cecil said. "To hell with the rest of it."

"What are you going to do with it?" I asked.

"You can have it," he said. "I'm done with this business."

"What am I supposed to do with it?"

"Hang on to it until this gentleman needs some more," he offered. "Easy money for you."

"Let's worry about the first half for now," I said.

I instructed the buyer's representative to meet me at the Don Pedro State Park fishing pier that night around eight.

"It's off Placida Road," I said. "There's a gate but it will be open. Take the dirt road and stay straight. It dead ends at the dock. There's room to turn around down there."

Cecil was ready to go, so we shoved him off the dock with instructions to anchor where he was before. Brody and I took the dinghy down to the dock before eight. A white van came down the dirt road right on time. It had no windows in the cargo area. The driver stepped out.

"You Breeze?" he asked.

I looked beyond him for any signs of followers or back-up. I studied him briefly. If he were an undercover cop, he was damned good at it. Brody was out on the dock looking for law enforcement vessels. She signaled that the coast was clear.

"Come with us," I said. "It's on that sailboat over there."

We took him out to Cecil's boat and he climbed aboard. Brody and I remained in the dinghy. We could hear them talking down below. The guy was low-balling Cecil, but Cecil had gotten his product cheaply. There was room to dicker. We heard the guy complaining how legal pot had driven down prices, even where it wasn't legal. Some of his customers had friends ship it to them from Colorado or even Maine. He'd never bought this much at once and didn't have enough money to pay a premium just because it was good Jamaican. Finally, they settled on a figure, with one catch.

He was prepared to take it right then. He'd come a long way. There was no one around to see. It was almost dark.

"Let's just get it over with right now," he urged. "I've got the cash in the van."

Brody and I looked at each other. Cecil shrugged.

"I'm ready if you are," he said.

"It's not high tide yet," I said. "You'll bottom out before you reach the dock."

"When is high tide," the buyer asked.

Brody looked it up. We had two more hours until the very top of the high. The buyer was visibly nervous. I stepped back and thought the situation over. It would be great if we could make the deal happen and be done with it as soon as possible.

I grabbed a boat hook from Cecil's boat and asked for a tape measure. I used a marker to denote the five-foot mark on the boat hook. I took the dinghy back to the dock and probed around it. The depth alongside was only four feet. It was six inches deeper at the very end of the dock. Within a few yards, it dropped down to six feet of water. I looked back at Cecil's boat. It had a high bow pulpit that extended out from the hull about three feet. I put it all together and came up with a plan. The sun was all but gone. It would be dark within fifteen minutes.

I went back and ferried the buyer to the dock. I instructed Cecil to aim directly for the end of the dock, not to pull alongside.

"You'll run out of water before you hit the dock," I said. "But you'll be close enough to transfer the bales. We'll help."

Brody and I went back to join the buyer and wait for Cecil.

"You sure this is going to work?" Brody asked.

"Pretty sure," I said. "Here he comes. Keep your fingers crossed."

The three of us watched in silence as the sailboat slowly approached the dock. We could see Cecil's white hair as he peered over the helm like an old lady peering over her steering wheel. He almost made it. The boat came to a grudging halt about ten feet short. Ten feet was too far to throw a fifty-pound bale.

"Fuck," said the buyer.

"Shit," said Brody.

"What do we do now?" asked Cecil.

I had to think quickly. A grounded sailboat was a curiosity, especially when it was where it clearly didn't belong. Boats passing by would come to render assistance. I got in the dinghy and instructed Brody to join me. I positioned it between the bow of Cecil's boat and the dock, tying a bow line to the dock and a stern line to Cecil's bow. Brody and Cecil switched places. She was to hand the bales to me. I would transfer them to the dock, and Cecil could help get them to the van. Instead of a bucket brigade, we formed a bale brigade. It went surprisingly quickly.

After the last bale came off, Brody and I joined the other two at the van. We made sure that Cecil got his cash. The white van drove off in a cloud of dust. We turned back to see Cecil's boat floating freely. The dinghy was still tied up to both the boat and the dock, so it didn't get far. At least now Cecil could motor off.

"I'm going to go back over and drop anchor again," he said. "I'm not traveling in the dark."

"You've still got five hundred pounds aboard," I reminded him.

"It's all yours," he said. "Come out and take it."

I looked at Brody for guidance. She was a law enforcement officer at heart, but she'd gone along with helping Cecil sell his dope. I had no idea what to do with such a large amount, but it was free for the taking. She shrugged.

"It's the least I can do," said Cecil. "I'd have really been stuck without your help."

"I don't know," I said. "I really don't know what to do with it."

"You're smart," he said. "You'll work it out."

"It's what you do, Breeze," said Brody. "Look at it as another problem to be solved."

"It will fit down in the bilge," I said. "I've had more than that down there before."

"Let's do it," she said.

"Okay then," I said. "We'll be out in the morning to take it off your hands."

"Bright and early," he said. "I'm itching to get out of here."

We said good night and motored back to the marina. I was glad that the job was done, but I was curious about what we'd do with our payment.

"Shit, Brody," I said. "Five hundred pounds. That's eight thousand ounces. What's an ounce of dope go for these days?"

"Up to three-fifty per ounce around here," she said.

"I can't do the math in my head," I said. "It's a couple million bucks at least."

"It's also eight thousand individual transactions," she said. "How many people do you know that smoke dope?"

"A handful," I said. "This will take some more thought."

"It'll work out," she said.

"Shit always works out."

Twelve

In the morning, we took *Leap of Faith* out of the marina to raft up with Cecil and relieve him of the rest of his weed. He had prepared for our visit by hanging a bunch of fenders on his port side. I nudged my boat next to his ever so gently. Brody tossed him lines and we all worked to secure the boat. There was no wind and he was anchored in a no-wake zone. There were no nosey fishermen nearby. We got to work right away.

Ten bales were moved from Cecil's boat to my boat and then safely stowed below in the bilge. I knew he was anxious to get moving, but he stopped me to talk before we left him for good.

"I want to express my deepest gratitude," he said. "You didn't have to do any of this. You're a good man, and I find that less and less these days."

"I'm not sure good men should be dealing in major weed transactions, but thanks," I said.

"There's one more thing," he said. "It's been on my mind. I know that we don't agree politically. We might even be on opposite sides of the spectrum, but you didn't let that stop you from coming to my aid."

"Why should I?" I asked.

"You've been away from the real world too long," he said. "There's a war going on out there, and I let myself get wrapped up in it. I became intolerant, and I should be ashamed. I let my tunnel vision affect my perception of others, as if politics was the only thing that mattered. You opened my eyes somewhat."

"You're just passionate about your beliefs," I said. "Just remember, the other side can be just as passionate, and many of them are good people."

"Good advice," he said. "I've learned a lot about myself on this trip. I can still sail. I can still taste adventure, but I'm afraid this is my last hurrah."

"I'm glad it worked out for you," I said. "Best of luck to you."

"Safe travels," Brody said.

"Enjoy yourselves, you two," he said. "You'll be in your eighties before you know it."

"Also good advice," I said.

"Enough with this," he said. "Shove off. I'm homeward bound."

We never saw him or heard from him again. I don't even know if he made it home safely. I like to think he's sitting in his rocking chair on his front porch in Georgia, fondly recalling all of his adventures. He's probably busy emailing his senators about legalizing marijuana or fixing health care.

Back at the marina, we simply ignored the fact that five hundred pounds of dope was stored below. Something would come up. We returned to our new-found life of luxury, enjoying the pool and the air conditioning. I kept forgetting that we owned a car. We could simply run to the store whenever we needed anything. The truth was, I wanted to make life easy for Brody. She'd been a great first mate. She rarely complained about the heat, the bugs, or the lack of amenities while living at anchor. Now though, she had it made. All I wanted was for her to be happy and to enjoy life. I'd never considered moving to a marina with any other woman. That had to mean something.

Everything was perfect, except for the continuing bad dreams. They nagged at me whenever I got too comfortable. It didn't happen every night, but when the dreams did come, they remained as vivid and alarming as ever. I still hadn't evened the score in the good deed count, and I doubted that I ever would. No one showed up at the marina asking for my help. No missions were pending. All I had to do was enjoy life, but the guilt was making it difficult. Finally, I had to confess to Brody.

"It's still bothering me," I admitted. "I'm still having the dreams."

"Let me find someone for you to talk to," she said. "I'm serious."

"I hate to admit weakness," I told her. "I thought I could deal with this myself."

"Seeking help isn't a weakness," she said. "It's human nature. We're a social species. We need each other."

"After my wife died, I never needed anyone until you came along," I said. "It interfered with my relationships. I discounted other people's value. It was all about me I guess."

"We're working that out together," she said. "Now let me help you."

"See what you can find out," I said. "I can't go on like this forever."

She came to me a few days later with a suggestion. She'd found a combat veteran who was helping PTSD sufferers in Saint Petersburg. He wasn't a doctor or psychiatrist, but he'd been there. He had extensive experience in Iraq, came home to an unfulfilling life, and returned voluntarily. He even had to change service branches in order to do it, as the Marines told him he was too old to fight. The Army had other ideas. He sounded like a tough son of a bitch. I decided that it couldn't hurt to talk to him, even though I'd never seen combat. His name was John Gunter. He promised an informal sit-down with no judgement. I told Brody to set it up.

"It's a long boat ride from here," I said.

"We've got a car, Breeze," she said. "It's less than two hours."

We went to see him at his house two days later. We found him at a picnic table in the yard. He was taking apart an old fishing reel. There was a bottle of Budweiser on the table and a cooler at his feet.

"Must be Breeze and Brody," he said. "Welcome."

"Nice to meet you, John," I said. "Thanks for agreeing to see me."

"My friends call me Jonnie," he said. "Jonnie Gee."

"I've got a reel just like that one," I said. "I abuse it pretty hard. Keeps on ticking."

"You fish a lot?" he asked.

"All the time," I said. "If it swims inshore, I can catch it."

"Me too," he said. "Looks like we've found common ground already."

He offered me a beer and I accepted, even though I disliked Budweiser. His wife came out and took Brody inside. We sat and talked fishing for thirty minutes. He was easy to talk to, with no pretense. I didn't feel like I was being psycho-analyzed. Eventually, he got to the point.

"So tell me what brings you to me," he said. "Brody says you're not a combat vet."

"I did a brief Army stint," I told him. "All of it in San Antonio."

"Fort Sam?" he said. "I heard it was like a college campus and full of pretty girls."

"Easy duty," I said. "But not all the girls were pretty."

"An ugly girl could give a man PTSD all by herself," he said, laughing. "Especially if she's mean."

"I'm surprised you can make light of the situation," I said.

"You gotta laugh, man," he said. "Otherwise you'll go crazy. Don't take shit too seriously."

"How'd you end up fighting over there?" I asked.

"Long story," he said. "First Lejeune, then Okinawa. Then I got out. I broke hearts and got my heart broken. Isn't that supposed to happen when you're young? I kicked all around Pinellas County, taking whatever life would give to me. After the twin towers went down I got all patriotic and tried to rejoin the Marines, but at thirty-six they wouldn't take me. I walked over to the Army Recruiter and told them I wanted a combat arms job. I did basic training all over again, this time at Fort Jackson."

"Must have been tough at that age," I said.

"It was like summer camp compared to the Marine Corps," he said. "I went to AIT to be a forward observer. Took part in the initial invasion of Iraq with the Second Brigade Recon Team. There was this op called Objective RAMS. I was in the third gun truck, and we got engaged. It took the gun company two hours to get to us. We had every kind of weapon we could carry on the trucks, AT4's, MK19 grenade launchers, fifty cals, and our individual M4s. After that is was a slum called Sadir City. Open sewage to your kneecaps, open air markets with flies all over meat and fish. Try doing a dismount patrol with shit up to your knees. Took fire almost daily, but there was nothing we could do about it because of the Rules of Engagement. Our main route to the other bases was gut clinching because of all the IEDs. Ask any soldier who has been in North Baghdad about Pluto, nothing nice to say about it."

"I can't imagine," I said. "But thank you for your service."

"There was more," he said. "We lost a lot of guys to IEDs, but I survived. I came back and got a job teaching soldiers about deploying overseas. It was supposed to be less stressful, and a cooling off period. Shit, I volunteered for deployment to Afghanistan on a team to train the Afghan Army."

"Why in hell would you do that?"

"Civilians don't understand why soldiers like deploying," he said. "The excitement and the adventure get to us. We come back stateside and nothing compares, except maybe being a cop or a firefighter. Some of us never fully come back. A lot of us are on prescription drugs for behavioral problems, yet pot, which is natural, won't be recognized."

"Funny you should mention pot," I said. "I've just had several conversations about the benefits of medicinal marijuana."

"I've seen it help a lot of guys," he said. "Sometimes it's the only thing that helps. I share what little I can get with the guys who need it, but money is tight."

"So let me get this straight," I said. "You are spending your own money to help vets who benefit from smoking weed."

"On a real small scale," he said. "This isn't a licensed facility or anything. I'm just a guy who came back mostly intact. I'm doing what I can to help those guys who are having a hard time adjusting. I wish I could help more of them."

That's when it all came together for me. I was sitting on five-hundred pounds of weed. I had no particular use for it, but Jonnie Gee sure did. I went there looking to help myself. Maybe I could leave there having helped him. In some strange way, the Universe had conspired to bring me here. The bad dreams, helping old Cecil out, the need to rid myself of the guilt, all led to this moment. I wanted to blurt out to him that I could help, but he spoke first.

"But hey, you came here to talk about your problems, not mine," he said. "What's been going on?"

"I killed a man with my bare hands," I said. "Down in Guatemala. I can't shake it. He haunts me in my dreams."

"What were the circumstances?" he asked.

"Short version is that an associate called me out," I began. "He challenged me. He moved in on my woman and my mission. He wanted to show me there was a new sheriff in town. I didn't want to fight him, I swear. But he forced my hand."

"And you killed him in a fair fight?" he said. "That's nothing to feel guilty about."

"I beat him," I said. "He was done and still alive. Then I kept beating him until he wasn't."

"What's the guilt really about?" he asked. "I've met men who would have walked away without a drop of remorse. The dude called you out. You won. Beats the alternative."

"It's about me losing control," I said. "That's not who I am. I went savage, man. You know what I mean?"

"I saw it happen a hundred times in Iraq," he said. "A man has his limits. Pushed beyond those limits he'll go berserk."

"But I'm not a soldier," I said. "I should have kept my cool."

"When I say a man has his limits, I mean every man," he said. "You included."

"What about you?" I asked. "Did it happen to you over there?"

"Not to sound proud," he said. "But when the bad guys are shooting at you, you reach your limit pretty quick. Killing them was exhilarating. Hell yeah I went savage. I needed to if I wanted to survive."

"That doesn't bother you now?"

"Not one bit," he said. "Seeing kids die was depressing, and will stay with me forever, but those other guys just needed killing."

"I don't think my victim needed killing," I said. "He was younger than me and in good shape, but he didn't come from the world I live in. I've been in life or death situations before, and so far I'm still kicking. He shouldn't have provoked me."

"That's right," he said. "He shouldn't have. He couldn't know how you'd react. He made a poor choice and he paid the price for it. The fault lies with him."

"He said as much on his death bed," I said.

"What else do you need?" he asked. "You've got to forgive yourself and move on."

"I guess I've been pretty hard on myself," I said. "I thought I deserved it."

"When it comes to coping," he said. "We all tend to be too hard on ourselves."

"How did you get over it?"

"Salt and light," he said. "Wash feet."

"I don't follow," I said. "What do you mean?"

"It's something a good man told me once," he said. "I went over to Jacksonville to the Five Star Veteran's Center to learn about dealing with PTSD. Jim was a religious man and staunch supporter of vets, especially the homeless. He would always say salt and light, wash feet. I took it as a reminder to help others as service to the Lord."

"I'm not a particularly religious man," I said.

"Never have been either," he said. "But this man was legit. He honestly wanted to help. He helped me so that I can help others."

"How do religious beliefs relate to PTSD?"

"He had a four step system to go by," he explained. "First was safety. Some guys might be suicidal or violent or homeless. Make sure they are safe first. Then there's affirmation. Like you being too hard on yourself. I tell you to keep fighting, that you're a good person. Encourage you to keep going and not to give up."

"I can see that," I said. "That's exactly what you did."

"Next is community," he said. "A lot of these guys withdraw from family and friends. They have me to talk to, but they also have the other guys that come here. I hook them up. They know there are others like them. They have friends."

"I've got Brody," I said. "But that's about it."

"You've got friends out there," he said. "You just don't let anyone get too close."

"I guess you're right," I said.

"Finally, there's character," he said. "Some of these men are on a downward spiral when they find me. They're on drugs, get into fights, losing wives and homes. I try to help them develop or rediscover the characteristics that will get them back on the right path. For Jim, that path was to be more like Jesus."

"Salt and light," I said. "Wash feet."

"You understand," he said.

"Understanding the path and following it are two different things," I said.

"You'll find your way," he said.

"I want to offer you the first step," I said. "I can help you, significantly."

"I'm here to help you," he said. "You don't owe me anything."

"You have helped me," I said. "But by some strange coincidence, I'm in a position to make a unique contribution to your mission."

"What kind of contribution?" he asked.

"If you accept, I can solve your pot supply problem for years to come," I told him.

"I can't afford very much," he said. "You a dealer?"

"Absolutely not," I said. "Not a user either. I just happen to have a boatload of the stuff, literally."

"How's that happen, or shouldn't I ask?"

"Let's just say I found it floating," I said. "All five hundred pounds of it."

"You want to give it to me?"

"It's all yours," I said. "You just need to come pick it up."

"Five hundred pounds?"

"Yup."

"I'll be damned," he said. "The Lord works in mysterious ways."

"I'm not sure how this all came together," I said. "But I feel like I'm supposed to be here doing this, right now. Does that make any sense?"

"It's the equivalent of washing a lot of damn feet," he said. "I'm most grateful."

"Me too," I said. "You made a lot of sense. I feel better already. Thanks."

We set a date and time for him to come pick up the weed. I rounded up Brody and we all said our goodbyes. Jonnie Gee was doing good work. I don't know if donating weed is doing God's work or not, but I felt good to be giving it. I told Brody to remember the name of the veteran's center in Jacksonville. We could afford to make a donation to them too.

Thirteen

I had Jonnie Gee show up after dark. The marina had several security cameras and I didn't want them to get a good look at the stuff we were moving. The docks weren't well lit and folks were rarely out after dark. We commandeered two dock carts and put the bales in black trash bags. One bale fit nicely in the carts. Five trips each and we had the whole load transferred to his truck. It was all over in less than five minutes. If anyone reviewed the night's activity, they'd simply see two guys making several trips back and forth with carts. One of those guys was a slip holder. There'd be no reason to be suspicious.

"You're like a weed angel," said Jonnie. "This is going to help a lot of people."

"Put it to good use," I said. "But keep a low profile. No need for you to get busted."

He put a tarp over his load, secured it quickly, and drove off.

Brody and I spent the next month living like marina queens. We never took *Miss Leap* out of the slip. We spent a lot of time at the pool. We took the dinghy to the beach. We attended the sunset dock parties almost nightly. We became friends with our neighbors. It was all very domestic and comfortable. The dreams were less frequent, and when they did happen, it didn't bother me as much.

Through the marina's gossip apparatus, I learned of some trouble brewing for a couple a few slips down from us. They had purchased an older sailboat with the idea that it could be restored and sold for a hefty profit. They got it for a few hundred bucks. The bones of the thing were good but it was a true project boat. They fell into financial difficulties soon thereafter and couldn't handle the cost burden of two slips and renovation. Mike seemed like a decent sort. He and his wife Mo loved to sail. They'd run a sailing school during the summer months, up in Maine. Mo was no taller than four and a half-feet tall, slightly round, and fully Irish. When she was drinking, she employed an exaggerated brogue that made everything she said sound funny. Mike liked to talk politics. His ideology was strictly conservative. It was a good thing that

Cecil was no longer around or we'd never hear the end of their bickering.

Word on the dock was that they were behind on the slip rent for the project boat. It was also becoming an eyesore, and the marina wanted it gone. I waited until I could catch the two of them alone and approached them about it.

"What are you going to do with that old boat?" I asked.

"You want it, it's yours," Mike said.

"If you can pay up our back rent you can have it," said Mo.

"What did you pay for it?" I asked.

"This old-timer gave it to us for five hundred," she said. "But the motor is seized up. It needs new sails. We bit off more than we can chew. She's a good old boat though."

"I'll give you the five hundred, and square up with the dock master on the rent," I said. "If you've got clear title."

"We do," said Mike. "What the hell are you going to do with it?"

"Fix it up and sell it, I guess," I said. "I wasn't looking for a project, but I'd hate to see you two get jammed up."

"Appreciate it, Breeze," said Mike.

"You really saved our bacon," said Mo. "We owe you some beers."

I was the not so proud owner of an ancient Tartan 33. I walked down and looked her over. Underneath the dirt and grime, I could see the lines of a once handsome vessel. I wasn't a sailor, but I loved all boats, especially old ones. They had character. Over the next week, Brody and I scrubbed every square inch of her. We had a diver come to clean the bottom. Brody found some cheap sails at a place in Sarasota. We had a sail cover made locally. The rigging appeared sound, but the lines all needed to be replaced.

The engine, a Universal 25, was one big ball of rust. I found a mechanic who promised he could rebuild it for less than a thousand dollars. It took Mike and me a full day to remove it from the boat. Once it was gone, Brody attacked the bilge with strong cleaners and lots of elbow grease. I painted the bilge compartment after it was dry. There were no cushions so we had new ones made. Brody was in charge of the interior decorating. We both worked long days in an effort to make the thing look acceptable to the marina, and any future potential buyers.

Brody did an internet search for similar boats for sale. We were surprised to discover that they were going for twenty thousand dollars and up. One that was in mint condition was listed at thirty-five thousand. We stood to make a tidy profit, which made me feel bad for Mike and Mo. They were on the right track. They just didn't have the capital to pull it off.

We got the engine back, and Mike helped me with the installation. It ran, but the transmission was toast. After throwing a wrench and more than a few curse words, it was time to take a break.

"Makes me glad that it's your problem and not mine," said Mike.

"Don't worry," I said. "I will win in the end. She won't beat me, then she'll make a fine boat for somebody."

Brody and Mo came down with cold drinks.

"You boys look frustrated," said Brody.

"Is the old girl kicking your ass?" asked Mo. "I always thought she was a contrary old bitch."

"Breeze is determined to tame her," said Mike. "Now it needs a transmission."

"I'll call around," said Brody. "What else is going to be wrong with it?"

"We haven't started on the plumbing and wiring yet," I said. "I might have to leave that to whoever buys her."

"She's going to need some instruments," said Brody. "How far are we going with this project?"

"We'll list it once we get the transmission working," I said. "If it doesn't sell right away we'll add some goodies."

"Are you keeping track of how much this is all costing?" she asked.

"Doesn't really matter," I said.

We ended up buying a refurbished transmission. It bolted right into place. The engine started. She went in and out of gear. Mechanically, the boat was whole. We took it for a test spin and made it back without breaking down or overheating, which was no small victory. Mike and Mo volunteered to get the lines and sails squared away. When they were done I asked them to take it out and sail it. They were thrilled with the opportunity. Brody and I helped them out of the slip and watched them motor down the waterway towards the sailing grounds.

"Do you think they're jealous that you got that thing in shape?" asked Brody.

"I hope not," I said. "I was just trying to help them out."

"It was a lot more work than you thought it would be, wasn't it?" she asked.

"Yes, but it kept me busy," I said. "I'm getting a little restless sitting here in a slip."

"I knew that would happen sooner or later," she said. "Do we have to leave already?"

"We'll hang around at least until we get the boat sold," I said. "Maybe longer. I'm okay."

It was clear that Brody didn't want to go back to living on the hook, at least not yet.

Mike and Mo came back in wearing big smiles. The shakedown cruise had been a success. The engine ran fine and the transmission worked fine.

"How'd she sail?" I asked.

"Like a dream, Breezy Boy," said Mo.

"We need to make a few adjustments," said Mike. "She's a little touchy. Reef her early if it gets to blowing."

"I'm not sailing her," I said. "I'm selling her."

"She's ready to go," said Mo. "I'd buy her if I could afford it."

"Me too," said Mike. "She really is a good boat."

"You want me to put it on Craigslist?" asked Brody.

"Not yet," I said. "Let's put a sign on her for now. I want to tinker with the plumbing and wiring."

"Not growing too fond of her are you?" asked Brody.

"The last thing we need is to own two boats," I said.

The truth is I wasn't ready to part with her yet. I was proud of the work that we had all done to give her new life. I wanted to find just the right owner for her. I don't know why but I had a feeling someone would turn up.

Three days later I was down in the bilge of the Tartan, installing a new pump. I came up for air and saw a young man standing on the dock, eyeing my vessel. He stood six feet tall, with blond hair and blue eyes. He was clearly fit and stood with a military posture. His hair was just starting to grow out and he sported a four-day stubble. I made him either for a soldier on leave, or a recently returned veteran.

"That's a fine looking boat," he said.

"Thanks," I said. "We've been fixing her up to sell her."

"I'm sure it's out of my price range," he said.

"You looking to buy a sailboat?" I asked.

"Yeah," he said. "I just got out of the Marine Corps, and I'm down here living in my truck, looking for a boat."

"What's your name, son?" I asked.

"Ames, sir," he said. "Daniel Ames."

"You don't have to sir me," I said. "The name's Breeze. So you're basically homeless, and you want to live on a boat."

"I don't consider myself homeless," he said. "I could be living with my father if I wanted to."

"Yet here you are," I said. "You should be starting a career, thinking about marriage and kids. Being a boat bum isn't for everyone."

"With all due respect, sir, being a boat bum is all I want to do right now," he said. "It's all I can think about. I just want the freedom for a while. I can work forty years at a job I hate later."

"You have some money saved up?" I asked.

"As much as I could," he said. "Won't last forever."

"It won't last at all if you keep looking at twenty thousand dollar boats," I advised.

"I was just poking around the docks," he said. "Saw the sign on her. Couldn't help but look."

I invited him aboard and offered him a bottle of water. He was very respectful, almost formal. I asked him about his service.

"I spent most of it in Japan," he said. "Took a sailing course and fell in love with it."

"Lasers, Sunfish, stuff like that?" I asked.

"Fun little boats," he said. "I got to instruct kids at a sailing school for a while. Beats dodging bullets."

"Did you see Iraq or Afghanistan?" I asked.

"I'd rather talk about Guam," he said. "Beautiful place."

He'd evaded the question nicely, so I let it slide.

We sat and talked for hours. He asked a lot of questions about the local waters and living aboard. He'd found the right person to get those questions answered. I doubted that anyone knew more about living aboard in the area. I enjoyed talking with him. Brody came looking for me later in the afternoon, so I introduced them.

"Very nice to meet you, ma'am," he said.

"Please, just call me Brody," she said. "And aren't you the handsome one?"

"He's fresh out of the Marines," I told her. "Looking to buy a boat and live on it."

"Breeze here is the expert," she said. "What kind of boat are you looking for?"

"A cheap one," he said. "I'm not afraid of a project. I need to stretch my money as far as I can."

"You plan to stay around this part of Florida?" I asked.

"At least until I get my sea legs," he said. "Depends on the boat I guess. How seaworthy it is."

Brody and I looked at each other in silent communication. We were in agreement. My premonition about the right person coming along had proven itself to be true. Here we had a fresh-faced young man, a Marine fresh out of the service, who was dying to own a boat.

"Why don't you stay for dinner," I said. "And you can sleep here tonight."

"Here on this boat?"

"Make yourself comfortable," I said. "We'll come get you when dinner is ready."

"That's awfully generous of you, sir," he said. "I'd like that."

"We're going to have to break you of that sir habit," I said. "Makes me feel like an old man."

"Sorry, sir," he said. "Habits die hard."

Brody and I returned to *Leap of Faith* and watched Daniel get a backpack out of his truck.

"What a nice young man," Brody said. "And a cutie to boot."

"I guess the Marines taught him some manners," I said. "Not like most kids these days."

"You're going to give him the Tartan, aren't you?" she asked.

"We'll see," I said. "He made a good first impression. Let's try to keep him around a few more days. We can get a better feel for him."

The next day I asked Mike and Mo to take the kid out sailing. They jumped at the chance. Mo and Daniel hit it off right away.

"Welcome home, Danny boy," she said. "And we thank you for your service to this great country."

"A Marine, huh?" said Mike. "I would have never made it through boot camp."

"I survived," said Daniel. "Overall it was a good experience. Made me grow up in a hurry."

"Now you want to be a sailor," said Mo. "You've come to the right place. Mike and I teach sailing, and we've already been out on the Tartan."

"I learn fast," said Daniel. "I appreciate any help you can give me."

"Let's raise the mainsail, laddy," she said. "We'll blow the man down and drink whiskey in the jar."

Lines were untied and the sail cover removed. The new engine fired right up and ran smoothly. Mo took the wheel and steered the Tartan out of the marina. Daniel stood with his hand on a shroud and a big smile on his face. I could picture him out on the open water, cranking winches as Mo hollered orders.

They were gone all day. When they returned, Daniel was at the helm. With Mo's instruction, he guided the boat smoothly back into the slip. Brody and I were waiting to catch the lines and tie it back up. Everyone was still smiling in spite of their newly acquired sunburns.

"Danny Boy is a natural, I tell ya," said Mo. "Got some Irish blood in him too. He'll make a fine sailor."

"The engine ran fine," said Mike. "Temp stayed normal. I can make a few more tweaks to the rigging, but other than that she's cherry."

"That was awesome," said Daniel. "I can't thank you enough. It was magical."

"Glad you had a good time," I said. "What do you think of the boat?"

"I love it," he said. "She jumps forward when the sails catch the wind. Responds sharply for her size. It's a lot different than a Sunfish, but I got the hang of it right out of the gate."

"He acts like he's been sailing for decades," said Mo. "He's got the knack for it, no doubt about it."

"Does it have enough room inside for you?" I asked.

"Plenty," he said. "I stretched out full-length last night and slept like a rock."

"Let's all go get a beer," I said. "I want to talk to Daniel some more."

We walked over to Leverock's and took seats at the bar. I got Daniel over in the corner so that I could ask him about his chosen lifestyle.

"What is it about living on a boat that attracts you?" I asked.

"Freedom," he said. "Not a lot of freedom in the Marine Corps. I went back home and the people drove me nuts. There's too much noise. Everyone is too busy. I just want to stay away from all that as long as I can."

"I can relate," I told him. "I've spent the last six or seven years avoiding people as best I could."

"So you don't think I'm crazy?"

"Unless I am too," I said. "You realize that slip costs five-fifty a month?"

"Oh I couldn't afford that," he said. "I'd anchor out."

"Near town or away from it all?"

"Away from town," he said. "Peace and quiet, good fishing."

"I know just the place," I told him.

"I don't even have a boat yet," he said. "I need to get back to looking."

"No you don't," I said. "The Tartan is yours if you want it."

"No way, man," he said. "You're joking me."

"No joke," I said. "I never really wanted it to begin with. You are the perfect fit."

"I can't accept," he said. "It's too much. You're being too kind."

"You can accept," I said. "You will accept."

"It's too good to be true," he said. "I'm supposed to be wary of that."

"No strings attached," I said. "Take her out of here tomorrow if you want to, but the rent is paid through the end of the month."

"I'll need electronics, and some safety gear," he said. "Can I stay here until I get her up to snuff?"

"So you'll take her?"

"I guess I will," he said. "I don't think I'm dreaming."

"Go put the rest of your stuff on board," I said. "Make her your own."

"Thanks, Breeze," he said. "I don't know what else to say. Just know that I'm grateful."

"We are all grateful for your service," I said. "Now go on and leave us old folks alone."

We shook hands and he looked directly into my eyes.

"Thank you, sir," he said.

Fourteen

Over the next few weeks, Daniel outfitted his new boat with everything he thought he needed. Every afternoon that the wind blew he was out there sailing. If Mo was around she'd catch a ride, but he was the captain of his ship. I put my favorite fishing holes in and around Pelican Bay into his new GPS. I plotted the only course that a six-foot draft vessel could use to get inside the bay, cautioning him about the tides. We talked about the Boca Grande Pass, tarpon, and sharks.

"There's sharks around there?" he asked. "I used to go shark fishing out of Ocean City."

"Big ones," I said. "Bulls and hammerheads. The Pass is the Tarpon Capitol of the World, but with tarpon come sharks.

"You'll have to come help me catch some of them," he said.

"I had a run-in with a big hammerhead not too long ago," I told him. "I was diving and he busted my ribs. I was lucky to get away."

"You didn't shit your pants?" he asked.

"You have to keep your cool in dangerous situations," I said. "Stay calm, find a way out."

I showed him on a chart the back way to the beach and the way to the Tunnel of Love. I pointed out Cabbage Key with its ten dollar cheeseburgers and four dollar beers. I gave him a brief overview of the area between Boca Grande and North Captiva, mentioning things to avoid, and things that he should know. I'd learned all those things the hard way, but now he could benefit from my experience. I even told him about the pot plants on Cayo Costa, and where the remains of my old rum still were on Punta Blanca.

"You think it will still work?" he asked.

"The still?" I said. "Sure. Just needs to be cleaned up, and you'll need some propane."

"I don't know how to make rum," he said.

"Maybe I can teach you someday," I said.

"I'll be ready to leave soon," he said. "You should come out with me and show me around."

"I'd love to," I said. "If I can pry Brody away from the marina."

"I'll work on her," he said. "She likes me."

Everyone liked him. Throughout it all, he remained consistently respectful and polite to all of us. He was quick to lend a hand when needed, and always cheerful. No gathering happened without someone mentioning what a fine young man he was. I went through his fishing tackle and showed him what worked and what didn't. I advised him on ground tackle too, and gave him some anchoring instructions. Brody took him to the Tax Collector's Office and helped him transfer the Tartan into his name. Mike and Mo tracked down a dinghy and outboard that he could afford.

The month was drawing to an end. A going-away party was planned. He bought some groceries and everyone on the dock donated canned goods to his pantry. Before the party started, Brody pulled me aside at the pool pavilion.

"You're not going to let that boy go out there by himself, are you?" she asked.

"I didn't think you wanted to leave," I said.

"He's just a kid," she said. "We've got to show him what's up."

"He's a Marine," I said. "I'm sure he'll be fine, if you'd rather stay here."

"Let's go with him," she said. "I know you're getting restless here."

Her willingness to leave the marina surprised me, but I jumped at the chance to get away. We loaded up with our own groceries and took care of all the incidentals that go with preparing to live at anchor. There was one last detail that needed to be taken care of. Daniel's boat had no name. Some of the liveaboards wanted to help him put together a renaming ceremony before he left. We were all waiting for him to pick out a name.

I gave it a lot of thought. I even used Brody's phone to search for ideas. He was a Marine. He had Irish ancestry. He had a tattoo of a trident on his leg. I twirled all those factors around in my head, but failed to think of anything significant. I kept mulling it over in my head until it came to me. I thought it was perfect. I walked down to the Tartan to make my suggestion.

"I've got it," I said. "You ready?"

"Ready," he said.

"Lion's Den," I said. "Like in Daniel in the Lion's Den."

He rubbed the stubble on his chin and nodded.

"That's rad," he said. "I fucking love it. Oops, sorry for the language."

"So it's settled?" I asked. "If so, I'll tell the others. They want to pitch in and get you a decal."

"Sure," he said. "It's perfect. Thanks."

I was happy to have solved his naming dilemma. I thought it was brilliant. I spread the word and everyone else agreed. Two of the girls went off to the local sign shop to have a decal made. They came back with a home port decal as well. It said Cape Haze, FL. Brody and Mo used Daniel's dinghy to clean his transom and apply the decal. They did a great job. It looked fantastic. Mike came down with a bottle of champagne and a handwritten script for the renaming ceremony. Daniel stood on deck and read it aloud, offering libations to the various wind and sea gods. We all applauded when he finished.

"I can't thank you all enough," he said to the gathered crowd. "You've taken me in as one of your own. Almost makes me not want to leave."

"There's a great big world out there to discover," said Mo. "Go while you're young enough to enjoy it properly."

"I'll miss you, Mo," he said. "You've been a big help with my sailing. And Breeze, I don't know how many times I can thank you, but it will never be enough."

"We're going with you," I announced. "Whatever you did to convince Brody, it worked."

"Awesome," he said. "This is the best day ever."

Brody gave me a soft jab with her elbow. She lit up with a dazzling smile.

"I'm so proud of you right this minute," she said. "There stands the adopted son of Palm Island Marina, on his cool old boat. He's about to have the adventure of a lifetime, thanks to you."

"Guess I needed a change from helping the ladies," I said.

"He looks up to you," she said. "Are you ready to be a mentor?"

"You sure you want him following in my footsteps?" I asked.

"You're the best man I know, Meade Breeze," she said. "And the perfect man to teach him."

"I'll do my best," I said.

Both boats left the marina the next day. We timed our departure to arrive at high tide. I went in first and Daniel followed close behind. We went slowly and carefully. He made it through the entrance without a problem but bumped bottom in the main part of the bay. I directed him on the radio towards the deepest hole I knew about. He dropped anchor in the center of it. We continued further south to our normal spot. I liked the kid but I still wanted some privacy. Brody and I had some catching up to do in the lovemaking department. We spent our first night at anchor tangled up like teenagers.

The first thing Daniel wanted to do the next day was fish for tarpon. We hadn't seen any rolling, but I knew that they often came through the bay on their way to and from the Pass. We jigged up some Threadfin Herring using a Sabiki rig and put them in a bucket. Daniel had rigged up a stout spinning rod with sixty-pound test braided line and eighty-pound test leader. It would handle a decently sized tarpon, but not the real big ones. We rigged the Herring under a float and carried it out away from the boat with the dinghy. The rod went into a rod holder and we waited.

Thirty minutes later we had our first strike. A six-foot tarpon exploded the bait and instantly broke our line. The fight didn't last two seconds, but it was now Daniel who was hooked.

"Did you see that?" he exclaimed. "That was some power."

"Looks like he broke your leader knot," I said. "Let me show you how to make a better connection."

I carefully instructed him in my method of attaching the main line to the leader. He watched closely and immediately duplicated my effort. We put out a new bait and waited again. I told him some stories about fighting tarpon on light tackle from the dinghy. An hour later we got another shot at a tarpon. This time the fight lasted ten seconds. The float went under, the drag screamed, the fish jumped, and it was over.

"We need bigger gear," Daniel said.

"You might be right," I said. "These are big fish. Let's give it one more try. Make sure all your connections are textbook perfect."

He worked with care and diligence to tie the perfect rig. We put out another bait and sat down to wait again. We waited all day. It was almost dark before something happened. The float went down and line started peeling off the reel. We had him on for five minutes, but couldn't regain any line. We never saw the fish. It didn't jump like tarpon almost always do. It dug down hard and simply pulled away from us until we ran out of line. There was a big fish out there somewhere trailing a few hundred feet of sixty-pound test braided line.

We were zero for three on big fish that day, but Daniel was thrilled. When he was tying rigs or fighting a fish, his focus was intense. He was more determined than ever to land one of those big fish.

"We need to chase after him," I said. "We'll tie off the dinghy loosely. Next time, hop in the dinghy with the rod. I'll drive. You fight the fish. We'll follow him around until he gets tired."

"Our plan gets a little better with each fish," he said. "We'll get one. I want a picture of me holding a monster tarpon."

The next day, we didn't have any herring around the boat. We jigged the Sabiki for an hour with no luck. Daniel put a piece of shrimp on a jig head and cast it towards a grassy patch. The first thing he caught was a catfish. He asked for the fishing pliers to get the hook out.

"Hold on a minute," I said. "Keep that catfish."

"What for?" he asked. "They're disgusting."

"Something my friend Diver Dan told me," I said. "The old-timers say the best bait for tarpon is a catfish tail."

"No shit," he said. "Let's try it."

We put the catfish in a bucket until he settled down. Daniel went about slicing his tail off just behind the dorsal fin. We employed a bigger rod designed for offshore fishing and a bigger hook. Our new bait looked like a side of beef hanging on the hook. Daniel took it out in the dinghy and dropped it a hundred feet off our stern. He carefully adjusted the drag and set the clicker to let us know when we had a fish on. We waited.

We brought Brody into the mix and assigned her a duty. As soon as we hooked something, she was to untie the dinghy. Daniel couldn't contain his excitement.

"I love this," he said. "I was born to fish."

"I can see that," said Brody. "You're like a little kid."

"We're gonna get him this time," he said.

I was keeping an eye on the float and saw it go under.

"Float down," I yelled.

Daniel moved to take the rod. The float stayed down and the line came tight. Bam, we were hooked up.

"Get in the dinghy," I said. "Turn that clicker off."

I followed him and started the motor. Brody untied us. The fish had taken more than half of our line. I accelerated after him as Daniel cranked the reel. After we regained most of the lost line I took the motor out of gear. The fish took us on a sleigh ride around the bay. It was a fast ride at first but eventually, we slowed.

Daniel started applying pressure. We got close enough to see what we had. It was a bull shark about eight feet long. It had to weigh close to two hundred pounds.

"Holy shit," said Daniel. "Did you see his teeth?"

"And we're in a rubber boat," I said. "We need to cut him loose."

We had nothing to cut the line with. We didn't have a camera or a phone to take a picture. Our plan had improved but we hadn't thought of everything. We ended up dragging the beast back to *Leap of Faith*. This revived the fish and the fight began anew. Brody came out with her phone and managed to get a decent picture before the shark caught the line on our running gear and broke free. We counted this as a victory as we'd handled the leader and controlled him.

"That was so friggin awesome," said Daniel. "But I need a break now."

"Good going, guys," said Brody. "That thing was huge."

"Sharks like catfish tails too," I said. "When you get done resting, put a knife and a camera in the dinghy."

"You want to keep fishing?" he asked.

"We haven't landed a tarpon yet," I said.

"Cool."

We spent the rest of the day hooking and fighting bull sharks. Our system had been perfected. We wore them out and cut them free. No more tarpon were hooked. Brody wanted to go to the beach the next day, and of course, Daniel took a fishing rod. He tried his luck in the surf while Brody and I looked for sand dollars. We sat up on the bridge that night, drinking beer and talking about our lives.

"This is going to be so cool," Daniel said. "I could definitely get used to this."

"It's not all fishing and beaches," I said. "It's thunderstorms and mosquitoes too."

"What do I do if a hurricane comes?" he asked.

"Good question," said Brody. "What do we do?"

"I haven't had to worry about it," I said. "Nothing has hit around here since I've been around."

"Shouldn't we have a plan?" she asked.

I pointed towards the southern end of Punta Blanca.

"We could sneak back into that little hole," I said. "Drop two anchors and tie off to the mangroves."

"Will two boats fit?" asked Daniel.

"If we arranged them right," I said. "We'd have to be the first to get there. I'm sure I'm not the only one that's considered it as a hurricane hole."

"What do we do with our poop?" He asked.

"Run off shore and dump it," I said. "It's perfectly legal."

"That won't be a problem," he said. "I'll be out there sailing anyway."

"Did you check your macerator pump?" I asked. "I didn't fool with it."

"What's a macerator pump?"

"Great," I said. "I'll come over and show you how it works."

"I've got a lot to learn," he admitted.

"You'll be fine," I said. "Pay attention to your boat. Investigate any different sounds. Keep the bilge dry and keep your eyes open. If something breaks, fix it right away. Don't let little problems turn into big ones."

"What if something breaks and I don't have the parts to fix it?"

"MacGyver it," I said. "Improvise however you can until you get someplace to find what you need."

"And if the head breaks you poop in a bucket, right Breeze?" said Brody.

"Whatever it takes to keep your independence," I said. "That's why we're here."

"Ah, freedom," said Daniel. "I can smell it in the air out here."

He stood up and put his arms out. He turned in a slow circle, breathing it in. I found it curious that a young person would want to separate himself from society. What had he been through that soured him on people? What was he running from? I knew what had driven me to seek solitude and freedom. It was something I never wanted to give up. He was too young to be a hermit. He'd want to find a woman. That would lead to a job and kids and a mortgage and all of the things that modern life required from a man. At least he had this chance to experience true freedom before all of that caught up with him.

Fifteen

One night I watched a Carolina Skiff sneak into a dead-end cove after dark. I couldn't see the driver well enough to identify him, but I clearly saw two red drums in the boat. When he came back out the drums were gone. All sorts of alarm bells went off in my head. I'd been in that cove several times. There was a trail leading inland, but it was overgrown and didn't really go anywhere. If those barrels were full, he couldn't have gotten far. I supposed he could have laid them on their sides and rolled them, but even that would be tedious. What the hell was he doing back there?

In the morning I decided to investigate. Daniel came over before I could leave.

"Did you see that skiff last night?" he asked.

"I did," I said. "Strange."

"You want to check it out?"

"I was just about to," I said. "Come on."

There was a post sunk into the mud at the trail head. We tied off and stepped ashore. We immediately noticed two wheel tracks in the dirt. The trail had been cleared recently. We followed the wheel tracks until we found the barrels. There was a cart designed to move them leaning up against a tree. There was also a hand-powered transfer pump and some lengths of hose.

"What do you think it is?" asked Daniel.

"Red means gasoline," I said. "Open one of them."

The threaded bungs were too tight to open without a tool. Daniel used his multi-tool to break one free.

"Yup, it's gas," he said.

I could think of no reason for a person to store gas on the island. It didn't make any sense. I didn't know what law was being broken exactly, but someone was up to no good. The pump and hoses suggested they would be filling something up. That had to be a boat. There were no cars or equipment on the island. But why not just go to a marina or even a gas station? We went back to the boat with no answers.

The skiff returned again that night, carrying two more drums. I asked Brody to search the local news for any extraordinary events, like Cubans on the beach or a string of arsons. Neither of those possibilities were in the news.

"Wait," she said. "Here's something interesting."

"What do you have?"

"A string of boat thefts in Punta Gorda Isles," she said. "They've taken five boats in the last two weeks. All stored in the water and not on lifts."

"If you steal a boat that doesn't have a full gas tank," I said. "You're going to need to fill it up before you run it to the Keys or Tampa or wherever they're taking them."

"We haven't seen any other boats go in there," she said.

"We just got here," I said. "That skiff has shown up two nights in a row. My guess is that some new thefts are about to go down."

"What do you want to do about it?" she asked. "Call the cops?"

"We could do that," I said.

"But that's not what you're going to do, is it?"

"You're pretty smart for a pretty girl," I said.

"Here we go again," she said.

"You think the cops are going to sit in the mangroves and catch these guys?" I asked. "They'll confiscate what's there and never catch anybody."

"We could wait until we see a boat go in there and then call," she suggested.

"It will take an hour or more for a boat to arrive," I said. "It will be after dark. I never see any type of law enforcement out here after dark."

"So you'll have to hold these guys for an hour while we wait for the cops," she said.

"If you have a better plan just say so," I said.

"Not really," she said. "What about the dinghy? They'll see it tied up when they come in."

"One of us will have to take it back out to the boat," I said.

"That only leaves two to guard our thieves."

"Guns," I said. "There won't be more than two or three of them."

When we met up with Daniel the next day, we discussed our plan. Brody was hoping that he would volunteer to drive the dinghy away from the scene. He was having no part of it.

"I'm going with Breeze," he said. "No offense, Brody, but I'm a Marine."

It struck me that I was the least qualified of our team. Brody was an FBI agent. Daniel was a Marine, and I was just a boat bum. It was nice to know that I had competent people on my side.

"Okay, okay," said Brody. "I'll drop you two off and wait by the phone."

"You make the call as soon as you see the boat," I said. "Then back us up with your pistol."

"I've got a weapon too," Daniel said.

"I've got my shotgun," I said. "That should be plenty."

"What if they run?" asked Brody.

"It's an island," I said. "Where are they going to go? The rangers can hunt them down in the morning."

"What if they run by boat?" she asked. "Say they make it back to the boat and take off."

"We need a way to block off the entrance after they get inside the cove," I said. "It's narrow enough."

"I can rig up a clothesline device," said Daniel. "Rope and chain with a pulley on one side. Brody sneaks in behind them and pulls it up off the bottom."

"That will slow them down until they cut the rope," I said.

"I'll use mostly chain," said Daniel. "It will lay down and let them cross over the top of it. The only rope will be where we attach it to trees or whatever."

"Sounds good," I said. "Go rig it up. We'll stake out the place tonight."

He borrowed a tape measure and went over to inspect the cove entrance. It was roughly fifteen feet wide for the first fifty feet or so. Inside, the cove opened up like a pond. It was a popular hangout for manatees. A piece of chain strung across the channel would stop a boat easily.

We spent the afternoon cleaning our weapons and going over the possibilities. The best outcome would be for them to surrender and let us hold them peacefully until help arrived. Law enforcement would catch them with a stolen boat, and the gasoline. If they ran on land, we'd let them go, and call the cops anyway. They couldn't get far and they wouldn't last long without food and water. If they made it back to the boat and ran, Brody would greet them on the other side of the chain. I reminded Brody that she'd have to lower the chain when the police arrived.

As darkness fell, we loaded up our gear, included rope to tie hands and lots of bug spray. We had a gallon of water and some granola bars. We each carried flashlights and our weapons. Brody beached the dinghy and Daniel and I scrambled out. We set up watch positions near the drums of gas and waited. It was four in the morning when we heard an outboard motor approaching. I had dozed off and Daniel woke me silently. We listened intently as the man made his way up the trail.

"Stop right there," I said, pointing my shotgun at him.

He froze and put his hands up. He looked around frantically. I thought he might make a break for it, but Daniel snuck up behind him and put him on the ground before he could move. The man's hands were bound within seconds.

We heard another boat coming. Was the chain up? Where was Brody? We remained still and listened. The boat entered the cove. We both snuck back down the trail to get a look. The first boat was the gas hauler. The second would be recently stolen. We watched the operator tie off to his partner's boat and climb across it. We heard him yell for Guiterrez.

"Where you at, man?" he said. "Fill me up so I can get out of here."

Our prisoner yelled to him.

"Run," he yelled. "It's a trap."

I hadn't thought of that possibility.

The second man scrambled back across the first boat and into the stolen one. The engine fired immediately and he backed away. He spun around and headed back out through the channel. I heard the sound of chain meeting fiberglass. Brody was on the job. I couldn't see what was happening, but I could hear the engine still running. If Brody were holding onto the rope, the boat would drag her into the water unless she let go.

"Come on, Daniel," I yelled, jumping into the remaining boat.

I fumbled around the console until I found the key. The outboard started and we made our way towards Brody. The thief was gunning his motor hard and fast, straining at the chain. Our dinghy was tied to the mangroves near the entrance. There was no sign of Brody yet. I fired a shot in the air. The thief looked back but didn't give up. Just then the chain fell away and the boat surged forward. He turned right out of the cove and headed towards the grass flats. We eased up to the entrance and saw Brody struggling to get out of the mangroves.

"I'm sorry," she said. "The rope broke."

"How did you hold him for so long?" I asked.

"I wrapped my end of the rope around a tree," she said. "We going after him?"

"You and Daniel stay here," I said. "Wait for the cops. Guard that other guy."

Daniel jumped out and waded over to Brody. I made sure they secured the dinghy before I took off after the thief. I didn't have to go far. He'd grounded on the flats. He had the motor trimmed up so that the prop was almost out of the water. It was throwing a long rooster tail as he tried to work his way into deeper water. I stopped short of his position, dropped an anchor over the side, and slipped over the stern with my shotgun in hand. I walked up to him in knee deep water until he saw me coming. I pointed my weapon at him and yelled for him to shut down.

It was eerily quiet without that motor running. I saw blue flashing lights over by Useppa. The cops were on the way. They had to run beyond Punta Blanca and use the north entrance unless they wanted to end up grounded too. I saw more blue lights coming from the direction of Boca Grande.

"The jig's up, buddy," I said. "Just chill."

There was nowhere for him to go. He shrugged and looked resigned to capture. I walked back to the skiff to use the radio. I hailed approaching law enforcement on channel sixteen. I explained that we had two men in custody and where each was located. The boat coming from Boca Grande arrived first and went into the cove where Brody and Daniel waited. The second boat came my way. I waved them down with the flashlight.

Before they could reach me, I put my weapon in the boat and tried to hide it under some rope. I didn't know how they'd react when they saw a man with a gun standing in the water. They used a loud speaker to instruct both me and the thief to put our hands up.

"That's your boat thief over there," I told them.

"We really discourage vigilante acts," he said. "But boat thieves in Florida are like cattle thieves in the old west."

"This boat is theirs too," I said. "I commandeered it to run this guy down."

"How'd you get out here?"

"I've got a dinghy in that cove that your fellow officers went to," I said. "Two of my friends are there with it."

"What boat are you on?"

"That trawler right there," I said. "You passed in on the way in."

"Leap of Faith," he said. "I've seen you out here a lot."

"I didn't like these guys using the island to steal boats," I said. "This is my home."

"Let me make a suggestion," he said. "Take that boat back where you found it. Gather up your friends and go back to your boat. We're going to pretend that you had nothing to do with this."

"Fine by me," I said. "Take all the credit you want. I'd prefer it that way, actually."

"Call us first next time," he said. "I mean that."

"Will do, officer."

"Go on. Get out of here."

I slowly made my way back across the bay and into the cove. The police boat was tied up in the only available spot, so I tied the skiff to it. I put my shotgun in the dinghy and walked up the trail. There were two officers. One was handcuffing our gas hauler. The other was taking pictures of the barrels and equipment.

"Officer Johnson told us to make sure you went back to your boat," said the photographer.

"We'll all be happy to get out of your way," I said. "Come on. Let's go."

The three of us walked back to the dinghy in silence. As soon as we started motoring away, we all spoke at once.

"That was some hairy shit, man," said Daniel.

"I was worried that the thief would shoot at me," said Brody. "I didn't want to have to shoot him."

"Me neither," I said. "I didn't see any signs of a weapon."

"Fucking thieves," said Daniel. "Can't stand them."

"I think their thieving days are over," I said.

"The folks of Punta Gorda can rest a little easier," said Brody. "Thanks to you."

"Hey, it was a real team effort," I said. "You two did great. Brody, you should have seen Daniel in action. He disappeared. I didn't even see him until he had that dude on the ground."

"Like a ninja," said Daniel.

"You boys have had your fun," said Brody. "Can we stay out of trouble for a little while now?"

"Let's go get some sleep," I said. "We'll go to the beach later."

The mission to halt the boat theft ring was a success, but I brooded over missing an important detail. We should have brought something to gag the first guy with. Duct tape would have done the trick. If the second guy had turned left instead of right, he'd have gotten away easily. He had a fifty-fifty shot at escape, but he made the wrong choice. It was dumb luck that I'd caught up to him. If I was going to continue to play these dangerous games, I'd have to be sharper. These crooks didn't have guns. The next ones might.

Sixteen

The next day, we watched as every law enforcement agency that could float arrived on the scene. There were boats from the Sheriff's Department of both Lee and Charlotte Counties, the FWC, the Coast Guard and the Punta Gorda Police Department. There was even a helicopter hovering over the cove. I doubted that the manatees appreciated all the traffic.

Brody followed the news coverage of the next few days. The only mention we got was that a private citizen had tipped off law enforcement. Our names were not mentioned, as the cops didn't even ask us for identification. The arresting officers looked like heroes, which was fine by me. Initially, there was some confusion over what to charge the gas hauler with. They first charged him with loitering in a state park, which technically closes at sunset. They later discovered that he was wanted for various parole violations. They kept him in jail with no bail for his previous crimes. The second guy was charged with grand theft and also jailed.

Our merry little band went back to fishing, sailing, and beach combing. Daniel had gotten frustrated with working the tides to get out into the Gulf and back. If he left at high tide, he couldn't return until it was high again. This made for long days, and nowhere to run in a storm.

"Where can I go with deeper water that's close to the Gulf," he asked me.

"Fort Myers Beach has a deep channel," I said. "And it's right on the Gulf. You can be sailing in a few minutes."

"You want to go down there with me?" he said. "Show me around?"

"We'll need some provisions soon anyway," I said. "Why not?"

"Where do we anchor?" he asked.

"I usually get a mooring ball," I told him. "But you can anchor in the backwater near my friend Diver Dan. Brody and I can sneak you into the showers."

I showed him the chart for Fort Myers Beach and checked the tides for the next few days.

We had an early morning high coming up. The tide didn't matter getting into Matanzas Pass. It was recently dredged and plenty deep. He wanted to sail so I advised him to go outside in the Gulf. Attempting to sail in the ICW was not advised, unless motor sailing. Brody was happy to return to civilization so we made plans to relocate.

We let Daniel get a head start on us. His route was longer than ours. We took our time leaving the bay and began the easy trip south. The weather was fine and the traffic was light. We saw dozens of dolphins along the way. One of them gave us a thrill by jumping multiple times. They seemed to like *Miss Leap*. We left the ICW at Saint James City and turned west to go under the Sanibel Causeway. We crossed the open water between Sanibel and Estero Island and looked out for *Lion's Den*. We saw sails several miles out, but couldn't tell if it was him or not.

We picked up a mooring ball in the back field without a hitch. Brody was good at grabbing them. Not long after we got settled in we saw Daniel motor under the Matanzas Bridge. He stayed in the channel, motored past us and headed for the anchorage where Diver Dan stayed. Robin and One-legged Beth both used to be back there too, but Dan was by himself these days. We had pre-arranged to meet at the Upper Deck for dinner.

I introduced Daniel to Jennifer and asked her to take care of him whenever he came to town. It would be good for him to have a friendly bar to visit. Over the next few days, we introduced him to Diver Dan and Robin. We all gathered up on the third day to go to the grocery store.

"I want you two packing heat," I said.

"For the grocery store?" asked Brody.

"Yeah, what's up?" asked Daniel.

"There are some idiots that like to give me a hard time," I explained. "They always hang out behind the market."

"What sort of a hard time?" asked Brody. "If it's bad enough to require weapons."

"I had to rough one of them up to retrieve Beth's leg," I said. "That started it. I found them on my boat one night after that. I outsmarted them by untying their skiff and letting it drift away. Then one night I came back drunk and depressed. They got the jump on me and I didn't have the wherewithal to fight back. They got tired of punching me eventually and left."

"Seen them since?" asked Daniel.

"Luckily, no," I said. "But I haven't been into their lair either."

"Sounds like Breeze in the lion's den," he said.

"Mostly toothless lions," I said. "But guns will stop them from bothering us."

"I got your back," he said.

"Me too," said Brody.

We took two dinghies in order to carry all the groceries. Brody and I tied up first. The mangrove mafia were in their usual spot. I waited for Daniel to tie up before stepping onto the dock. The big one spoke first.

"You looking for another ass whooping?" he asked. "Because we'd be happy to oblige."

He took a few steps towards me. In a flash, Brody had her gun barrel jammed into his temple. She twisted one of his arms behind his back and led him back to the log he'd been sitting on.

"Got yourself a little lady to fight your battles for you?" the smallest one said.

"He's got me too," said Daniel, showing his gun. "So think twice."

"I suggest you remain seated while we conduct our business," I said. "Or you can leave if you want."

"Go ahead and get your stuff," the big one said. "We won't fool with no guns."

"You won't fool with our dinghies either," I said. "That would be very unwise."

He shrugged and we walked up towards the market, taking a stray shopping cart with us.

When we came back they were still there. As far as I could tell, they lived right there in that spot, sleeping in the mangroves at night. Our dinghies were untouched. Daniel kept on eye on them while we loaded the dinghies with groceries. Before leaving, I turned to address the three bums.

"You'd do well to consider this a truce," I told them. "I've got enough help here to settle the score with you three, but I'm giving you a pass. We won't be through here without weapons, but if you leave us alone we'll leave you alone."

"I reckon we've tangled enough," the big one said. "Bygones be bygones."

"Smart move," I said. "You boys have a nice day now."

It was a small victory to get our supplies without bloodshed. Those old boys had too much time on their hands. It makes you wonder how folks end up that way, and how they lack the will to change their situation. I'd been poor as dirt at one time, but I didn't give up. I scratched and clawed and did whatever I had to do to improve my lot in life. I recognized that my situation was due to my own poor decisions. The world didn't owe me a damn thing.

Daniel brought up the rear as we exited the canal. The bums made no move to follow us. He went back to his boat and we went back to ours.

"I'm not sure I like having to carry a weapon just to go shopping," said Brody.

"We can go to the Publix down by Snook Bight," I said. "But it's a long ride. Besides, I wanted to serve notice to those dudes while I could."

"You mean while you had the fire power," she said. "You'll always have me. I'm sure

Daniel will want to go his own way sooner or later."

"Are you good with him being the third wheel in the meantime?" I asked.

"Of course I am," she said. "I like him a lot, but there's something going on that I can't quite put my finger on."

"With Daniel?"

"He's holding back something," she said. "Suppressing his feelings about something."

"It's what men do," I said. "He'll work it out."

"I think you should talk to him about it," she said. "See what's eating him."

"Neither one of us is the touchy feely sort," I said.

"Just talk to him, man to man," she said. "He's following in your footsteps. He'll listen to you."

"I'll try," I said. "If, and when, the time is right."

Later that week Daniel asked me to help with a wiring issue. I hated twelve-volt wiring, but I had a little experience so I agreed to help.

Brody stayed behind so we could have some man time.

"What's the issue," I asked as soon as I boarded his boat.

"The bilge pump," he said. "The float switch works, but when I flip the manual override nothing happens."

"Did you check the fuse behind the switch?" I asked.

"I didn't know it had a fuse," he said. "The positive wire from the battery has a fuse. It's good."

I showed him how to unscrew the little knob that the fuse sat behind. I pulled out the fifteen amp automotive fuse and inspected it. It looked good. I pulled up the hatch that gave access to the pump itself. I'd never gotten around to rewiring it. Daniel hadn't either. Someone had used wire nuts to make the connections. This was asking for corrosion and eventual failure. I twisted on the nuts and told him to try the switch again. The pump sprang to life.

"All this needs to be redone," I told him. "Use butt connectors and shrink wrap over the top of that."

"I don't think I have those," he said.

"There's a hardware store further down the beach," I told him. "We can go tomorrow and get what you need."

"You want a beer?" he asked.

"Close enough to five o'clock," I said.

We sat in his cockpit and drank our beers. We went over the list of things that he should have aboard but didn't. He really couldn't afford everything that I thought he should have, so we prioritized. I saw my chance to initiate further discussion.

"So tell me why you really want to live like this," I said.

"This is even better than I thought it would be," he said. "I'm loving it. It's just what I needed."

"Why the big need to get away?" I asked. "How old are you anyway?"

"Twenty-three," he said.

"Twenty-three and life has already beat you down?"

"Maybe I just saw some truths earlier than most," he said.

"Did something happen to you overseas?"

"A lot of shit happened, man," he said. "But coming back home was what made me mad."

"The killing didn't bother you?"

"Not as bad as seeing my buddies get killed," he said. "Or seeing some kid get blown to bits. It's not hard to shoot some raghead that's trying to kill you. You just do it. I just did what I had to do to survive."

"Then you came home," I said.

"Don't get me wrong," he said. "I love America. I fought for my country, but people here can really suck."

"No argument there," I said. "What specifically are you referring to?"

"Over there," he began. "Those people got nothing. Shitting in the street, eating sand all day long. Mother fuckers shooting at everything that moves all night long. They're lucky to get one bowl full of fly infested rotten meat for dinner. No running water, let alone cable TV with mother fucking Netflix too."

I just let him talk. I took his free use of the F word as him being on a roll.

"Kids my age," he said. "Bunch of fucking spoiled pussies. Shallow as a dried up mud puddle. Can't tell you who the Vice President is. Can't find Iraq on a map. Nose stuck in a damn phone all day. They disgust me. People your age ain't no better. Here's my McMansion and my expensive car. It's all bullshit. None of it is real."

"I think this is where I'm supposed to give you a pep talk," I said.

"Won't work, man," he said. "I can't live like that."

"Did you feel this way before you became a Marine?"

"I was eighteen years old," he said. "I didn't know shit. I only went in because my sister did. Couldn't let my sister be a bigger badass than me."

"Where is she now?"

"She's up in Arlington," he said. "Cushy job. Doing her own thing."

"What about your father?"

"He's in Ocean City," he said. "I love him and all, but there's no future there for me."

"You're awfully young to be so cynical," I said. "Sure, a lot of it is pointless, but you make your way as best you can."

"Spend a year in some middle-eastern hellhole," he said. "Pick one. Syria, Afghanistan, all fucking hot fucking hellholes. There's some pointless bullshit. Then come back here and see these idiots with their smart phones and two hundred dollar shoes whining about how unjust everything is. Everybody is a victim. Transgender bathrooms. Sanctuary cities. Safe spaces. Politicians fucking up healthcare to hell and back. What the hell are we doing?"

"That's a big adjustment," I said. "I'll grant you that."

"I can't adjust," he said. "I just can't do it. I almost signed up for another tour, just to get away."

"But you decided to sail away instead."

"Best decision I ever made," he said.

"So it wasn't the death and destruction over there that soured you?"

"I think about it," he said. "Have some bad dreams sometimes. If I think about it too much it makes me want to kill some assholes."

"I have to tell you something," I said. "I killed a man. It took me a long time to deal with it. Still am, I guess. Brody has killed a man too."

"I gotta hear these stories," he said.

"Not today," I said. "But I know a guy you should talk to. He helped me."

"Not until you tell me about killing somebody," he said.

I told him the whole sad saga of Bobby Beard. I left out none of the details. I was honest with him and honest about my shame.

"Sounds like he had it coming," Daniel said.

"We all got it coming, kid."

Seventeen

Over the next days, Brody and I talked to him about how we dealt with our issues. He had only one desire; to forget all about it and live free on his boat. He didn't want to open up about his own issues. To be honest, I wouldn't have either if it hadn't been for Brody. I'd chosen the same lifestyle, run from my problems and lived alone in the wilderness, just to avoid dealing with life. I'd evolved over time, though.

I had cared for Holly deeply and I learned that life wasn't just about me. When I found Brody, or rather when she found me, I rediscovered what it meant to truly share your life with someone else. I got personal satisfaction out of helping my friends when they were in need. I still didn't fit in with modern society, but I was making better use of my life, in whatever small way I could. Daniel was too young to be a hermit.

It took some doing, but I convinced him to go see Jonnie Gee. We loaded up both boats and headed back to Palm Island Marina. Daniel decided to anchor out at Don Pedro rather than pay for a slip. We took a transient slip by the pool. Our old friends were surprised to see us. They were even more surprised when Daniel arrived in his dinghy.

"You're a vision I hold in me dreams, Danny boy," said Mo. "Couldn't stay away from old Mo, could ya?"

"How's the *Lion's Den* faring?" asked Mike.

Daniel fielded their questions with grace. In polite company, he refrained from sounding like a Marine. No F-bombs were dropped. We all drank beer and swapped stories by the pool until sunset. Brody called Jonnie and spoke for a few minutes before handing the phone to Daniel. He walked away from us for privacy. He was gone for fifteen minutes.

"I'll go talk to him," he said. "Wants me to stay for a few days, meet some of his buddies."

"You can take our car," I offered. "We're good on groceries for now."

"All I ever do is thank you for stuff," he said. "Sooner or later you'll have to kick me out of the nest."

"You'll know when it's time," I said.

Daniel left the next morning for Saint Petersburg. Brody and I felt like parents sending their child off to summer camp for the first time. I took his dinghy out to his boat and Brody picked me up. A dinghy trailing behind a boat meant that someone was aboard. We hoped it would keep any petty thieves from taking advantage of Daniel's absence.

We washed *Miss Leap* while we had access to unlimited water. We spent the afternoon in the pool. We spent the evening making love. Three days later, Daniel called and announced that he'd be staying a few more days. If we needed the car he'd get Jonnie Gee to help him return it. We told him to keep it and to enjoy his time. Jonnie himself called a few minutes later to explain. He'd arranged to hold a barbecue for a bunch of the guys he'd counseled over the years. He was cooking a whole pig, buying a keg of beer, and putting in horseshoe pits. Daniel was getting along fine, but he really wanted to introduce him to some of his fellow soldiers.

Brody and I soaked up some more sun at the pool, drank more beer, and made more love. She absolutely loved being in the marina. Daniel could stay as long as he wanted, as far as she was concerned. I was enjoying the air conditioning myself. We were getting spoiled again.

"What do you think they're doing up there?" asked Brody. "I hope they aren't banging bongos and dancing around a fire or some crazy shit."

"Probably just drinking beer on the tailgate of a pickup truck," I said. "Shooting the breeze. Telling tales of their time in whatever middle-eastern hellhole they served in."

"And smoking dope," she said, laughing.

"Shit, I didn't think about that," I said. "Our little boy is probably getting high right now."

"You know he's not a little boy," she said. "He's probably done it before."

"I'll stick with beer and rum, thank you," I said.

"You've done real well not drinking too much lately," she said. "Still trying to hone your situational awareness?"

"I don't know," I said. "I feel pretty safe here. I think it's because I have you. I'm not filling up emptiness anymore."

"That's the most gracious thing anyone has ever said to me," she said. "You never cease to surprise me."

"I surprise myself sometimes," I said. "When did I become so loving and charitable?"

"Sometime after I hunted you like a dog and put my claws into you," she said.

"So that's where the marks in my back came from," I said.

"Don't you forget it."

Daniel showed up a few days later. He was sporting a five-day beard and a duffel full of dirty clothes. Brody took his bag and made a beeline for the laundry room.

"How'd it go?" I asked.

"Good," he said. "I'm just tired. Need some rest."

"You want me to take you out to your boat?"

"If you don't mind," he said. "I've had enough of being around people for right now."

"I understand," I said. "Come on. Let's go."

I dropped him off and left him alone. I went back to the marina and found Brody at the pool, waiting to flip Daniel's laundry.

"Where's he at?" she asked.

"Took him to his boat," I said. "He wanted to be alone."

"What did he say?"

"Nothing, just that he'd had enough of people for a while."

"Is he okay?" she asked.

"Said he was tired."

"You didn't ask him about his trip?"

"He wanted to be left alone, so I left him alone," I said. "I've been there."

"Clamming up doesn't help," she said. "He needs someone to talk to and you're all he's got."

"I'm sure he and Jonnie Gee did plenty of talking," I said. "That's what he went up there for."

We waited most of the next day for him to show up at the marina. By the time happy hour rolled around Brody couldn't contain herself any longer. She packed me a cooler of beer and forced me to go out to talk to him. I found him kicked back on the foredeck with his legs crossed in front of him.

"Permission to come aboard," I said. "I brought beer. And I've got your laundry."

"Permission granted," he said.

I climbed up and sat down in the cockpit, cracking a cold one. He came back and sat across from me. I handed him a beer.

"Brody's worried about you," I told him. "Made me come out and check on you."

"I'm good," he said. "Jonny was pretty cool. Introduced me to some of his friends. It was a useful trip."

"Did you gain any new understanding of things?" I asked. "Thought about what you want to do next?"

"I still want to stay out here as long as I can," he said. "I think I want to go off by myself for a while."

"I can appreciate that," I said. "But it's just the two of us right now. Tell me what's on your mind, son."

He began fidgeting with a winch, taking the line off, rewrapping it, and tightening it back up.

"Couple of things," he began. "Seeing those other vets brought back some memories. Most of those guys are way more fucked up than me. I'm going to be okay. I promise you that. I promised myself that. Being a Marine means keeping the macho dial at ten at all times. Who can drink the most? Who can lift the heaviest weight? Who can fight the best? Say one sensitive thing and you're labeled a pussy. I bought into that for a while, but I saw some of them break when the shit hit the fan. I thought those guys would be the ones who couldn't adjust. I didn't break, man. I survived."

"You're going to be fine," I said.

"Jonnie Gee called it survivor's guilt," he said.

"You didn't do anything wrong by surviving," I said.

"I see that now," he said. "We talked it all the way through."

"So are you on the road to putting it behind you?"

"I can deal with it," he said. "I feel better about it. It's people in society that I can't deal with. Like I said before, I don't understand what is wrong with everyone. The really important things don't matter to them, but they get all worked up about the silliest things."

"I get it," I said. "Out here we care about catching a good fish, or a good sunset. Feeling the rhythm of the sea. Being close to nature."

"That's the good stuff," he said. "I'm at home out here."

"I'm the last person who would argue with that," I said. "But you'll need to earn some money eventually. You'll get lonely, want to meet a girl."

"I realize that," he said. "But I need this time."

"You don't need to ask my permission," I said. "You are your own man."

"I feel bad leaving you and Brody," he said. "You've been better to me than my own father. I owe you."

"This boat is not a debt," I told him. "You don't owe us a thing."

"It's not just that," he said. "You've taken a real interest in me. You've taught me so much. You hooked me up with Jonnie Gee. I repay you by taking off."

"You taking off for good?"

"I'll be back," he said. "I'm just going to go hole up someplace where nobody else is. Work on my head. Be one with my boat and with nature. Give me a month. Then I'll come back and you can help me figure out what to do next."

"Sounds like *Walden's Pond*," I said. "A young man could do a lot worse."

"I knew you'd understand," he said.

"You going to say goodbye to the rest of them?"

"Can you do it for me?" he asked. "Let me ride off into the sunset."

"Sure kid," I said. "You know where to find us."

I went back to the marina to break the news to Brody. She was impatiently waiting.

"The bad news is he's gone," I said. "The good news is he'll be back in a month, so we're stuck here until he gets back at least."

"Wait, what? Where's he going?"

"To be alone," I told her. "You get to keep your pool and air conditioning for another month."

"I trust you, Breeze," she said. "But I can't believe you let him go."

"How was I supposed to stop him? Besides, I think it's a good idea."

"You would," she said.

"He's going to be fine," I said. "No doubt in my mind. He'll come back more independent, and stronger. He says we can help him decide what to do next."

"I'll have to give that some thought," she said. "It will be impossible to get him off that boat."

"He'll need money," I said. "A job and a car."

"He's going to hate that," she said.

"That's why he's doing what he's doing," I told her. "We can't take that away from him."

"We'll help him get started won't we?"

"If he needs it, or accepts it," I said. "I wouldn't be surprised if he makes it without our help."

"I suppose you're right," she said. "As usual."

We resigned ourselves to Daniel's absence and went about the business of being marina bums. We hung out at the pool nearly every day. Happy hour started at five and carried on until sunset. I took care of boat chores and Brody took care of the shopping. We shared the cooking duties and ate out often. The month quickly passed by with no word from Daniel. After five weeks we began to think he wasn't coming back. After six weeks we got worried. Brody called his phone every day but got no answer.

"We've got to go look for him," she said.

"He could be anywhere," I said.

"Isn't that what you do?" she asked. "Track people down?"

"Maybe he doesn't want to be found," I offered.

"He can tell us that after we locate him," she said. "Come on, Breeze. Put your thinking cap on and figure out where he is."

"There's not a lot of options for a boat with his deep draft," I said. "We know he went south when he left here."

"Let's go," she said.

We left right away. We kept binoculars handy to scope out any anchored sailboats we might encounter along the way. It was only a two-hour ride to Pelican Bay, during which we saw none. We entered the bay and didn't see him there either. I checked behind the bar, up along Punta Blanca, to no avail. We looked in the hurricane hole at the south end of Punta Blanca too. We came back out and circled around to pass by Useppa Island and Cabbage Key. There was no sign of him.

We continued traveling south past Captiva and Sanibel. We checked the anchorage off St. James City. We looked across the water way near Ding Darling. He wasn't at either place. It was getting late so we crossed San Carlos Bay and motored into Fort Myers Beach. We idled slowly through the mooring field looking for *Lion's Den*. We found it anchored up in the back not far from Diver Dan's boat. There was no dinghy tied to it. We dropped the hook close by and settled in.

It wasn't long before Diver Dan came over in his skiff. He knew where Daniel was. It wasn't good news.

"They've got him in the city jail up in Fort Myers," he said.

"What for?" I asked.

"Three counts of assault, one with bodily injury," he said. "Can't afford the bail."

"Why didn't he call us?" asked Brody.

"He's embarrassed," he said. "Plus he couldn't accept any more of your money."

"What's his plan?" I asked. "Rot in jail forever?"

"He's asking for a public defender," he said. "Take his chances in court."

"What the hell happened?"

"He went up to Topp's Market and those assholes jumped him," said Dan. "Guess he whupped all three of them pretty good. Somebody called the cops."

"And they arrested Daniel for defending himself?" asked Brody.

"Bad optics," said Dan. "The sympathy is all wrong on this. Crazed Marine abuses three homeless guys."

"How much is the bail?"

"Fifty grand," said Diver Dan. "Judge said he's clearly a flight risk because he lives on a boat. Like I said. It just looks bad."

"How do we get to him?" I asked.

"Take the trolley up town," he said. "Ask the driver to drop you close to the courthouse."

"We'll go first thing in the morning," I said. "Thanks for filling us in."

"I wanted to call you," he said. "But he insisted I didn't get you involved."

"Stubborn ass," I said. "We'll be fully involved now."

"His dinghy is still behind Topp's," he said. "The bums haven't been around lately."

Brody and I retrieved Daniel's dinghy and tied it off to his boat. We ate dinner and turned in early. Brody was worried sick. I assured her that he would be okay. In the morning, we used the dinghy dock at Matanzas Inn to catch the trolley. The driver dropped us off within two blocks of the courthouse. We inquired about the bail for one Daniel Ames. The clerk looked surprised. She made a call and we were soon greeted by someone from the prosecutor's office.

"What is your relationship to the defendant?" he asked.

"Friends and bail bondsmen," I said. "We'd like to see him released as soon as possible."

"That would be up to the judge," he said.

"The judge set the bail, and we're here to pay it," I said. "Simple as that."

"This case is getting a lot of attention," he said. "All the wrong kind for your friend."

"He has a solid case for self-defense," I said. "We'll get him a good lawyer."

"What if he decides not to appear?" he said.

"Then I'll be out fifty grand," I said.

"Fair enough," he said. "There's some paperwork to attend to. I'll get the clerk started on it and notify the judge."

"Thank you," I said.

"You know you could pay a real bondsman a percentage of the bail," he said. "If you've got collateral to put up."

"None of us owns any property," I said.

"Suit yourself."

After he left I explained to Brody why I didn't want a bail bondsman involved. If Daniel didn't show up, a bondsmen would send someone looking for him. I had my doubts that Daniel wanted a trial, which would mean legal fees and more indebtedness to us. She was dubious. She wanted me to make sure he made it to trial, to prove his innocence. I reminded her that we'd recently pulled weapons on the same victims. Who knows what they might say in court.

We got to talk to Daniel a few minutes before he saw the judge. There was no time for him to argue. We were there to get him out and he was coming along. He stood before the bench with his military posture and treated the judge with the utmost respect. He had no prior arrests. He was a veteran. The judge had no choice but to accept payment of the bail and grant his release. We exited the building quickly and caught the trolley back to the beach.

"I could have worked this out on my own," said Daniel. "Now I owe you more than I can ever repay."

"I couldn't let you sit in jail," I said. "Brody would have killed me. Mo too."

"We've all been worried to death over you," said Brody. "Are you okay?"

"I'm fine," he said. "I was great until those assholes decided to come after me."

"I know they aren't exactly tough guys, but how'd you manage to take all three of them?"

"I went all Tasmanian Devil on them," he said. "Feet, fists, and elbows. Didn't take much to drop any of them."

"One of them is hurt pretty badly?"

"Brittle bones I guess," he said. "Didn't hit him that hard."

"We'll start looking for a good lawyer tomorrow," said Brody.

"What's that going to cost?" asked Daniel. "Another fifty grand? I can't take it."

"We've got more money than you realize," I told him. "It's not going to hurt us."

"That's not the point," he said. "You gave me a boat. You bailed me out. Where does it end?"

"Think it over," I said. "Decide your next move carefully. You've got sails. You can disappear at any time, or you can stay and face the music."

"The TV and papers have made me out to be a monster," he said. "I'm screwed."

"Let's go out to the boat and drink it over," I said. "Always helps me figure things out."

"I could use a cold beer or six," he said.

Eighteen

We were sitting on *Leap of Faith* drinking beer when Brody's phone rang. I could hear a hysterical woman on the other end.

"It's Holly," said Brody, handing me the phone. "I can't make out what she saying."

"Calm down," I said. "Take a deep breath and try again. Where are you?"

"Key West," she said. "Shit, Stock Island I mean."

"What's going on?"

"Tommy's mom died," she said. "He wanted to come back to Florida. I agreed to come with him. But Breeze, he didn't make it."

"What do you mean he didn't make it?"

"We were almost to Key West when he dropped dead," she said.

"Damn," I said. "What is it exactly that you need?"

"Fucking shit, man," she said. "I'm on a big rusty shrimp boat, anchored in the channel in

Stock Island, with a dead body and several million bucks stashed all over the place. I don't know what to do."

"If you call someone about the body, they'll figure out it's Tommy," I said.

"Then they'll confiscate the boat and everything in it," she said. "Millions, Breeze."

"I know, I know," I said. "Let me think a minute."

Holly was in quite the predicament. The boat itself would be recognized, sooner or later. Tommy's body wouldn't keep for long in the heat of the Keys. She was freaking out down there.

"Take him out twenty miles," I instructed. "Weigh him down and give him a burial at sea."

"I can't do it," she said. "I can't touch him. Help me."

Brody and Daniel were giving me inquisitive looks.

"Burial at sea?" asked Brody.

"It's Tommy," I said. "Holly needs help."

"Then let's go help," said Brody.

"Holly, we'll leave tonight," I said. "We're in Fort Myers Beach. We'll be there by this time tomorrow."

"I can't believe this is happening," she said. "I'm sorry, Breeze. One more time. I can't handle this by myself."

"We're on the way," I said. "Hang in there for one more day. Maybe get some ice on him if you can."

"Fuck, fuck, fuck," she said. "Icing a dead body on a rusty tub. What the fuck?"

"Do it," I said. "We'll be there soon."

I turned to Brody and Daniel, who had already heard my end of the conversation.

"You coming with us?" I asked Daniel.

"What about his court date?" Brody asked.

"It hasn't been set yet," I said. "Might be back in time, might not."

"I'm going with you," Daniel said. "Let's get out of here."

"You taking your boat or leaving it here?" I asked.

"I'd like to take it," he said. "I've never been to the Keys. It would be cool to have my boat down there."

"We're going to run seven knots, nonstop the whole way," I said. "You won't get to sleep. Can you keep with us and stay awake?"

"I can do seven if the wind is right," he said. "And I can stay awake. Stayed awake for seventy-two hours during the Crucible."

I took him to his boat and dropped him off.

"Get her ready right now," I said. "As soon as we see you pull up anchor we'll roll out."

"Five minutes," he said. "I'm good. Go on back."

I started the engine and let it warm up. I punched in a course for Key West while Brody secured things below. Daniel started hauling in his anchor. Brody took the helm while I raised ours. *Leap of Faith* and *Lion's Den* left the harbor together. We were in for a long night. I had Brody to spell me at the wheel. Daniel did not.

Fortunately, the weather was cooperative. There was enough breeze to keep Daniel sailing at a good clip, but the seas were manageable. I couldn't have planned it better. The moon was nearly full, giving us some light to navigate by. The sun came up before we reached the Key West Bell. We went down the Northwest Channel and through Key West Harbor. We used the cruise ship channel until we were clear of any hazards, then turned east for the Stock Island entrance channel. Daniel's sails came down and we entered the channel mid-afternoon.

Holly had anchored in the only open spot big enough to accommodate the big shrimper. She was indeed partially in the channel. That would draw the attention of law enforcement eventually. We anchored well outside the channel, taking care to make sure we had a good hook set. I turned on my handheld VHF and tuned it to channel seventy-two, Holly's preferred channel.

"Get over here," she said. "I'm about to go crazy."

We used our dinghy and picked up Daniel before heading over to Holly. It was a lousy time to introduce the two of them, so we just got down to business. I found Tommy on a cot that he kept to the right of the helm. Holly had stuffed two big black trash bags with blocks of ice and placed them on top of him. A white sheet covered his head. His feet stuck out at the bottom of the cot, betraying his condition. All he needed was a toe tag.

Brody had seen death before. So had Daniel. We all just stood there in a moment of silence.

"How much fuel does this thing have left?" I asked Holly.

"Should be close to two-hundred gallons," she answered. "We can get out pretty far."

"Spare anchors and rope?" I asked.

"Port side locker," she said. "Behind the compressor."

I sent Daniel and Brody to dig out whatever they could find to weigh Tommy's body down. Holly was trembling like she'd seen a ghost. She had in fact, been sitting with one for two days. I hugged her and held her tight for a minute.

"This will be over soon," I assured her. "Everything will be all right."

"Because shit works out," she said.

"Always," I said. "Now fire this thing up. We've got a ceremony to perform."

The old shrimper was named *Coming Home*. On this trip, it was Tommy who was coming home. He'd spent his life on the ocean, looking for treasure. He'd found it more than once. He was a strange man, but damn good at what he did. They say he was the smartest man ever to hunt for gold. I'd come to know him late in his life, after he'd lost a few steps. He still found his treasure. Holly and I were both the beneficiaries of his finds. I was glad to have known him. It was just too bad that it had to end this way.

We chugged along in a southerly direction for several hours. No one was talking. Holly was chewing her nails and twirling at a dreadlock. Brody and Daniel had fashioned a rig of chain, rope, and anchors to send Tommy to the depths of the sea. With an eye on the fuel gauge, we stopped and drifted about thirty miles south of Key West.

Daniel and I carried Tommy out on deck. We worked to fasten him securely with chain and anchors. He was stiff, which hampered our efforts. When we were satisfied with our work, we propped him up against the gunnel. I asked Holly if she wanted to say anything. She started crying.

"I don't know what to say," she said. "I'm sorry. I don't have any words but thank you, Tommy. Rest in peace."

Brody and Daniel shrugged. It was an awkward moment. I didn't know what to say either, but someone needed to give a proper send off. I decided to recite the Twenty-third Psalm. I don't know how but I'd remembered the words since childhood.

"The Lord is my shepherd: I shall not want. He maketh me lie down in green pastures, he leadeth me beside still waters. He restoreth my soul: He leadeth me in the path of righteousness for his name's sake. Yea, though I walk through the valley of the shadow of death, I will fear no evil: for thou art with me, thy rod and thy staff they comfort me. Thou prepares a table before me in the presence of mine enemies: thou anointed my head with oil; my cup runneth over. Surely goodness and mercy shall follow me all the days of my life, and I will dwell in the house of the Lord forever."

Everyone said amen. I nodded to Daniel. Together we slid Tommy up and over the side. He sank to the bottom in two hundred feet of water. The deed was done. Brody comforted Holly while I went back to the helm. I turned the old shrimper around and headed back the way we'd come.

I didn't want to go back to Stock Island. There wasn't enough room for us to anchor there. When Holly settled down, I asked her about the money. She had millions in two huge duffel bags under a bunk. It wasn't exactly hidden. She told me that Tommy had stashed his in various hiding spots throughout the boat. She didn't know where they all were. I decided to make locating all of Tommy's cash a top priority. I also decided to anchor off Key West while we searched.

There was plenty of room in the deep water off Fleming Island. Smaller vessels dotted the shallower areas. The shrimper had plenty of chain and a huge anchor. We could make do in the deep water for a day or two, while I figured out what to do next. The four of us set to tearing Tommy's boat apart looking for money. I crawled around in the bilge. Brody opened up compartments and checked for false bottoms or backs. Holly scoured the hold and engine room. Daniel went through the top decks and equipment lockers. By the end of the first day we'd recovered three million dollars in cash. We knew he had more, lots more.

We conferred that evening over beers, discussing where we'd looked and where we hadn't. We mapped out a plan for the next day's search. Holly was anxious to leave.

"How am I going to get this boat back to Guatemala by myself," she asked.

"Can't you just fly back?" asked Daniel.

"Excuse me, airline lady," said Holly. "I'm going to need to check these huge bags of cash."

"It's actually illegal to take over a certain amount of cash out of the country," said Brody.

"*Another Adventure* is sitting down there waiting for me," said Holly. "I've got to go back. I can't sit here on Tommy's boat with all this money."

"I'll go with you," said Daniel.

Holly looked at me as if to say *who is this kid anyway?* I realized that they hadn't been properly introduced.

"Holly, meet Daniel Ames, United States Marine Corps," I said. "He's a sailing fool, fishing machine, and nice young man. Daniel, this is Holly. She is also a sailing fool, expert diver, and a very nice young woman. She's also filthy rich."

"I can see that," said Daniel. "Nice to meet you, Holly."

"You're a sailor, eh?" said Holly. "I saw you come in on that Tartan."

"I sailed it down here by myself," he said. "First time to the Keys."

"Sorry about the chaos," she said. "Nice to meet you too."

"I'd be happy to go down with you," he said. "Just fly me back."

"What do you think, Breeze?" she asked. "Is he capable?"

"I can't think of any reason why he couldn't do it," I responded.

"I can," said Brody. "He's got a court date coming up sometime soon."

"I'm thinking I'm not going to show up for that," said Daniel. "I can make this trip, check out Guatemala and Belize. Maybe take my own boat back down there."

"I haven't agreed to anything yet," said Holly.

"What choice do you have?" asked Daniel.

Holly looked at me, silently asking for my help yet again.

"Oh no," I said. "No way we're going back to Guatemala. Take Daniel. He'll be a big help."

"I'm against it," said Brody. "He needs to go back to Fort Myers."

"The choice isn't ours to make," I told her. "It's his, and part Holly's I suppose."

"I'll take him," said Holly. "He's right. If you won't go I've got no other options."

"We are not going," I said. "I'll help you plan and get ready. We'll need to get *Leap of Faith* and *Lion's Den*."

"I know the owner of a boatyard there," said Holly. "We'll put Daniel's boat in a slip. I'll pay for it. We can probably tie off this old junker for a day or two provided I buy fuel from him."

"Let's find the rest of that money and set this thing in motion," I said.

"I'm going to be giving you and Brody some of what we find," said Holly. "You helped as much as anyone to earn it. I'll never be able to spend it all."

"I guess I won't say no to that," I said.

We spent another day digging through Tommy's boat. Sometime that afternoon Holly let out a whoop.

"Jackpot," she yelled.

We came to see what she'd found. Hidden in plain sight, amongst some luggage and trash bags full of clothes, sheets, and blankets, was a huge duffel full of cash. We'd all walked right by it dozens of times. We found more duffels just like it, full of Tommy's belongings. We emptied his stuff and used these duffel bags to store the rest of the cash. We had four of the over-sized packs stuffed to the gills with green. Holly handed one of them to me. It was surprisingly heavy.

"Don't argue," she said. "Just take it."

I did as she suggested, more than doubling what money I already had. I had no idea where I was going to keep it, but that was a problem to be solved at a later date.

Holly called the yard in Stock Island and arranged for a berth for the shrimper and a slip for Daniel's boat. We made the short trip the next day. I used the dinghy to haul my newly acquired big old bag of cash out to *Leap of Faith*. Brody helped me drag it to the forward berth where we covered it with blankets and towels. I needed to start locking the boat again.

Holly and Daniel stocked up on groceries while I checked over Tommy's boat for potential problems. I found an EPIRB but had no idea if it was still working. There was a life boat strapped to the forward deck. The dates on it indicated that it was still valid. It likely needed an oil change, but it had but one more trip to make. I checked the belts and found them in good condition. It was far from a luxurious vessel, but Tommy had kept it in good mechanical shape. I suspected Holly would just ditch it somewhere once she got back to her own boat. There was no further need for a treasure hunting ship.

Holly had brought along a small device called an InReach. It used satellites to determine your position. One could send out text messages or even an SOS signal. Rescuers could locate you with the corresponding GPS coordinates that were sent with the message. I made her put Brody on her contact list. We planned to stay in the Keys until we knew Holly and Daniel had made it to Guatemala safely. We could keep an eye on *Lion's Den* until Daniel returned.

Tommy's GPS had a course clearly marked for the trip back and forth from Guatemala and Florida. Holly had run through those waters several times. We'd first traveled together when she crewed for me on a trip back from Grand Cayman. We'd also traveled to Costa Rica and back together. I had confidence in her ability to navigate those waters. Daniel would learn a lot on the trip. It would be a nice little adventure for him. I spoke to Holly about giving him some money to get started on his life after he got back. She agreed that if he was an able first mate, she'd overpay him for his services. She made no mention of it, but I thought she liked him well enough.

Nineteen

Holly was in a hurry to get the old shrimper away from prying eyes and to get back to her boat. Daniel was eager to go as well. I'd been over all the key maintenance items and instructed Daniel what to look out for. Everything was operational. There was no need to worry about their safety.

Holly and I investigated the weather forecast for the next few days. There was an area of interest in the Gulf of Mexico. The various weather sites we visited gave it little chance to develop into anything tropical. The wind shear in the Gulf was thirty knots or more from the north. The only way it could develop was if it tracked due south. All the spaghetti models showed it heading towards the Big Bend area of Florida.

Like me, Holly rarely dealt with Customs and Immigration when traveling overseas, but we made sure Daniel took his passport. He would need it to get back home. I couldn't think of anything else that needed to be addressed, so I signed off on the vessel's readiness. Brody and I stood at the dock and waved goodbye as Holly steered the old rust bucket out of the harbor. It was getting easier to say goodbye to Holly. Daniel had sealed his fate with the legal system in Florida. He'd miss his court date and a warrant would be issued for his arrest. I was out the bail money, but I didn't care. I was the last person who should lecture him on the topic. Besides, Holly had made Brody and me quite wealthy. I hoped that she'd be generous enough to Daniel that he could afford to live outside the law.

We walked down Front Street until we found the Hogfish Bar and Grill. We each ordered their signature sandwich and a beer.

"I wish he would have gone back to Fort Myers," said Brody. "Now he'll be on the run forever."

"All he has to do is not get arrested," I told her. "They won't search for him, and if they do, I doubt they'll find him."

"He's already been arrested," she said. "He was only gone a month before he got into trouble."

"I'll teach him to keep his head down," I said.

"You got arrested too," she said. "With all of your experience, eventually they caught up to you."

"I was engaging in activities that tend to draw the attention of law enforcement," I said. "I'll instruct him not to do that."

"What is it with you and the drug trade?" she asked. "You don't use. You're not a criminal. How'd you get involved in it?"

"It started innocently enough," I said. "I was starving. I got some seeds from a friend. I grew a little crop. It was enough for me to survive. I made a thousand bucks or so for three or four ounces at a time. That was big money for me back then."

"Somewhere it grew into something bigger," she said. "What happened?"

"It's a long story," I began. "I had real money waiting for me in the Dominican, but I couldn't afford to go get it. I took a job bringing in a load of dope for a big-time dealer. Then I couldn't get out. I got my money but I was an indentured servant to the man after that."

"How'd you get away?"

"He did some time," I said. "I ran the whole smuggling side of his operation while he was in jail, with the understanding that I could leave his employ when he got out."

"And he lived up to his word?"

"There is honor among thieves, and drug kingpins," I said. "We had a mutually beneficial arrangement for a period of time. That time came to an end."

"I'm glad that was behind you when we met," she said. "Things may have gone differently."

"You tolerated me helping Cecil," I said. "You didn't have to."

"I wanted to watch you," she said. "Follow how your mind works. Then you gifted your half to a good cause. Impressive."

"New leaf and all that," I said. "Just trying to help."

We went back out to the boat before dark, watched the sunset, and turned in early. Brody rewarded me for my good deeds in the way only a woman could. We had developed a pattern of having less sex whenever Daniel was around. That was enough reason for me to let him go with Holly.

We were having coffee the next morning when Brody's phone pinged. It was a message from Holly's InReach.

SOS. Mayday. Going down. Need help. Mayday.

It was a hell of a way to wake up. I instructed Brody to click the link provided. They were west of Cuba, well out of Cuban waters. They had a life raft, if it functioned. They were young and resilient. I could get to them in half a day if I left immediately. The Coast Guard could get to them much quicker. I wondered about the money. If the Coasties picked them up, what would become of it?

We wasted no time. The engine was running and the anchor was up in minutes. Brody called the Coast Guard while I steered us out into the Atlantic. The chopper from Key West was out of service. They would dispatch one from Miami. A search plane would be underway within the hour. I made a waypoint for Holly's last known coordinates. I tried to calculate set and drift, but my mind wasn't cooperating. I wasn't in a full panic, but I couldn't think the problem through. The wind was out of the north. The current would carry them to the east. If they floated long enough, they would drift to the south of Cuba towards the Caymans.

I never pushed my old boat very hard, but this time was an exception. I pushed the throttle forward, increasing the rpms. *Miss Leap* managed to achieve a speed of eight knots. The engine growled instead of purring. I'd eat up twice the fuel, but I didn't care. I had to get to Holly and Daniel as quickly as possible. We plowed ahead with a sense of urgency.

Two hours out we got another ping from Holly.

In the raft. Floating. Boat gone.

They weren't far from the first position, but a lightweight raft would drift much quicker than a steel-hulled boat. I made a slight adjustment to our course and motored on. At least we knew they were still alive. Brody had tears in her eyes.

"Is this as fast as we can go?" she asked.

I pushed the throttle forward again. *Miss Leap* didn't like it. We ran at nine knots for a few minutes before the temperature started to rise. I back off the throttle until the temperature stabilized. Eight and a half knots was the best we were going to get out of her. The radio crackled to life.

"Coast Guard C-130 to motor vessel Leap of Faith. Please advise your position."

I relayed our position and told them we intended to pick up the crew from *Coming Home*.

"We can get a cutter underway. It's kind of what we do, sir."

"Send the cutter out if you want," I said. "But I'm responsible for two souls and I intend to take them aboard. Locate them and advise of their position."

"If they are in imminent danger," he said. "The chopper will pick them up."

"Understood," I said. "But we're still going after them."

"Will advise at first sighting," he said.

"Roger that."

Our speed was faster than my old boat had ever traveled. Normally, I was happy with six or seven knots. On that day, it felt like we were crawling. We made steady progress though. The C-130 found them first. A flare was launched from the life raft. We didn't see it but the plane did. They directed the chopper in for a closer look. The crew was alive and well. The seas were heavy but not dangerously so. The cutter turned around. The plane made another pass and confirmed two souls on board the life raft, before heading back. The chopper stayed on station until we arrived.

I positioned my vessel alongside the raft. Brody tossed a line. Daniel caught it and pulled the raft until it was almost touching us. Three big green duffel bags were lugged over the side. Two wet humans dragged themselves aboard. The chopper inquired as to the condition of the rescued crew. Holly didn't look right, but she insisted she was okay. Daniel reported no injuries. Something was going on with them, but it wasn't the time to discuss it. We told the chopper that all was well.

Brody took them inside while I got us underway again. The chopper tailed me for an hour. I finally convinced him that there was no medical emergency. He veered off and headed for Miami. I was worried about Holly. I engaged the autopilot and went below to see what was going on. Holly was white and weak. I could see no signs of injury.

"What happened?" I asked.

"Lightning," Holly said.

"We took a direct hit," said Daniel. "Couple of thru-hulls blew out. When the water started coming in she split open."

"We popped the life raft," said Holly. "Thank God it inflated. Daniel tossed the bags and grabbed the InReach."

"That was about all we could do," Daniel said. "It went down fast."

"I'm just glad you're both alive," said Brody. "Holly, are you okay?"

"Dan says I was out," she said. "Like in dead. He gave me CPR. Saved my life."

"Why didn't you let the chopper pick you up?" Brody asked.

"The money," she said. "We knew we'd lose the money if the Coast Guard got us."

"What if we hadn't gotten to you?" I asked.

"I knew you'd come," said Holly. "It's what you do. Save my ass."

"We'll get you to a hospital as soon as we get back," said Brody. "Don't argue."

She was in no state to argue. We laid her down and covered her with blankets. Daniel stayed with her while Brody and I returned to the bridge. My boat was carrying more cash than most banks, and two lucky adventurers.

I ran at a leisurely pace on the return trip. I let the engine purr. I hoped I'd never again have cause to make it growl. I patted the dash with my hand. *Good job, Miss Leap.* We motored on all night, arriving in Stock Island after the sun was up. Holly felt better after eating some breakfast. Her color had returned to normal. Brody still insisted that she get checked out. I locked up my floating Fort Knox and took everyone to shore.

We got a ride to a walk-in clinic in Key West. Brody took Holly inside while Daniel and I waited on a bench outside.

"What really happened out there?" I asked him.

"The second the lightning hit, Holly was out," he said. "She went down like a sack of flour. She had no pulse, wasn't breathing. I started CPR right away. While I was working on her I could feel the boat starting to list. As soon as she came around, I ran up front and deployed the raft. I dragged it down the low side where Holly was. By the time I got back to her the gunnel was even with the raft. I knew we didn't have much time. I slid her over the rail and into the raft. I was about to shove off when she spoke. All she said was *the money*. I went back aboard and carried two bags at once. I thought my back would break. When I went back again for the third bag, I was waist deep in water. I jumped in the raft and untied us. We hadn't drifted more than a hundred yards when the boat disappeared."

"You kept your cool," I said. "I'm damn proud of you, and grateful. Holly has been an important person in my life. You deserve a medal."

"The CPR was just instinct," he said. "I've been trained. The rest of it was remembering what you told me, to keep calm when the shit hits the fan. Work out the problem and solve it."

"I couldn't have reacted any better myself," I said.

"After the excitement was over and we were just floating, I started to worry," he admitted. "But Holly said you'd come for us. How'd you get to us so fast?"

"I was ready to leave at the first sign of trouble," I said. "And I pushed the old boat hard, too hard. I ran a course to a point where I thought you'd drift to, not to where you sent the Mayday."

"I wouldn't have thought of that," he said.

"What's next for you?" I asked. "Probably still time to make that court appearance."

"Brody probably thinks it's a sign that I'm supposed to go back to Fort Myers," he said. "I've got other ideas."

"Like what?"

"I'm going to take Holly and her money down to Guatemala on my boat," he said.

"Jumping right back on the horse, huh?"

"What are the odds of a catastrophe happening while trying to make the same trip twice?" he asked.

"Are you sure your boat is capable?"

"It will be the ultimate test for her," he said. "She's stout. I've got a good feel for her now. I can do it."

"What about you and Holly?" I asked. "You've only known her for a few days."

"We kind of bonded out there in that raft," he said. "That's something neither of us will ever forget. Now I feel responsible for her. I want to do this."

"Doesn't hurt that she's pretty and rich," I said.

Brody and Holly came out, interrupting our conversation.

"Fit as a fiddle," said Holly. "Takes more than a million volts to take this girl out."

"EKG was fine," said Brody. "Blood pressure, heart rate, all that stuff was good."

"Let's celebrate over lunch," I said. "And have a little talk about the future."

We walked down to Front Street and took a table at Two Friends Patio. Two chickens pecked at the floor and a pigeon landed on a neighboring table. We ordered drinks and looked over the menu.

"Lunch is on me," proclaimed Holly. "I owe all three of you. Don't think I don't appreciate everything you've done for me. I'm lucky and I know it."

"Have you given any thought to settling down somewhere?" asked Brody. "You can buy a nice little house. Live a life of leisure."

"And die of boredom," Holly said. "No way, no how, no never."

"What do you want to do?" asked Brody. "That money makes anything possible."

"That money makes sailing around the world a reality," she said. "If I wreck on a reef I'll just buy another boat. I can eat and drink at the finest places, but it's the adventure that I'm really after."

"You're going to need some crew," I suggested, looking at Daniel. "And a way to get that cash back to your boat."

Daniel cleared his throat and took a drink of water. I watched him compose himself before speaking. He looked directly at Holly and gave it his best shot.

"I'd be honored to take you to Guatemala on my boat," he said. "I'd be thrilled to be your crew after that, if you'll have me."

It was like a marriage proposal. I'm surprised he didn't get down on one knee. Holly looked at me and gave me a knowing smile. It really was the perfect solution for both of them.

"I could rattle off a list of things wrong with this idea," said Brody. "But I won't. You two go see the world. Have a great time of it."

We all waited for Holly to respond.

"Daniel, thank you for your generous offer," she said. "I accept. As far as being my crew, let's see how we make out on the first leg of the trip. If you want to stay on, and I want you to stay, then it's a deal. If not, I'll reward you handsomely and send you on your way."

"I accept your terms," said Daniel.

"The meek shall inherit the Earth," I said. "But the brave get the oceans."

"Oohrah," said Daniel.

Twenty

The four of us worked together as a team readying *Lion's Den* for the passage. Holly paid for everything. She added radar, upgraded the GPS, and bought a new EPIRB. She purchased new batteries for her InReach device. New offshore life jackets were put aboard. She bought a gizmo that tests the tension on the rigging and tweaked all of it until she was satisfied. She even bought a spare mainsail, just in case.

During a break, I asked Holly if I could make a suggestion.

"When Brody and I came back up from Belize, we were having fuel problems," I said. "We made it into Grand Cayman to fix it. I think you should break up the trip into two legs. Stop off in Georgetown, rest up and take stock of the boat."

"Good idea," she said. "It will only add a day or two to the trip. I liked it there well enough."

"Grand Cayman sounds cool," said Daniel.

"Send us the okay signal when you get there," Brody said. "And again when you arrive in Guatemala."

"Will do," said Holly. "I think this old girl is ready. It's actually a nice little boat."

"Take care of it and it will take care of you," I said. "Don't take any chances. Get a good feel for the weather before you leave the Caymans."

"This ain't my first rodeo," Holly said.

"It's my first ocean passage," said Daniel. "I'm all about safety first."

"I'll have you burying the rail in thirty-knot winds in no time," said Holly.

"You make sure you get that boy there in one piece," said Brody. "We're kind of fond of him."

"He's the one saving lives and shit," said Holly. "I'm bringing him along to take care of me."

The four of us sat down to go over the weather forecast. I showed Daniel how to plot a course on his new GPS. We laid in a line to follow to Grand Cayman, and then to the Rio Dulce. The conversation turned to Holly's long-term cruising plans. Brody and I told them about our experiences in the Caribbean. We made suggestions on places to avoid and places not to miss. I'd never been through the Panama Canal, so she was on her own from there through the Pacific.

"What's your ultimate destination?" I asked.

"I want to spend some time in the South Pacific," she said. "Fiji, Tahiti, Bora Bora. Ultimately I'd like to get to Australia and New Zealand."

"Sounds like a hell of an adventure," I said. "*Leap of Faith* will never see the Pacific."

"So get a sailboat and come find us," she said, laughing.

"That's not going to happen," I said.

A silence fell over us. We both realized that we were facing another goodbye. We'd done a poor job of most of our previous goodbyes, but it was different this time. She had the means to make her dreams come true. I had no doubt that she'd follow through on her stated plans. She was comfortable with my relationship with Brody.

"Let's just say see you later," I suggested.

"Never say never," she said. "Who knows?"

"If you settle down somewhere," I said. "Give Brody a call. Let us know you're alive."

"I can do that," she said. "It's the least I can do."

"Safe travels, girl," I said.

"You too, Breeze."

I was walking down the docks towards the bar when Daniel caught up to me. I asked if he wanted a beer.

"Sure man," he said.

We sat at the bar and ordered two cold ones.

"There's a lot I want to say but I don't know how to say it," said Daniel.

"Don't worry about it," I said. "No need to get gushy on me."

"When I walked into the marina that day, I could have never guessed how things would turn out," he said. "I was just looking for a boat. Here I sit in the Keys, about to go on an epic adventure with the coolest chick I've ever met. And it's all because of you."

"You're welcome, kid," I said. "I couldn't have guessed how it would turn out either, but shit works out."

"Shit works out," he said. "Thanks, Breeze."

Brody and I didn't go to the dock to give them a send-off on the day they left. We'd said our awkward goodbyes already. Part of me was sad to see them both go. Part of me was jealous. Part of me was proud. Both of them had the skill and the balls to make it happen. I liked to think that I'd played a role in that. We all knew the risks that were involved, but I'd taught them both what I thought they needed to know. Mostly I'd taught them that shit works out. I knew they'd be okay. Whatever became of their trip and their relationship, they'd both land on their feet.

Lion's Den motored away from the dock and gave us a close pass. Brody and I stood on the deck and waved. Daniel and Holly turned their backs and mooned us. We watched them get smaller and smaller until they were out of sight.

"God, I hope they make it," said Brody.

"They will," I said. "Keep the faith."

"I'm going to be worried to death until we hear from them," she said.

"It's just you and me again," I said.

"And *Miss Leap*," she said.

We decided to hang around until we knew they were safe. The waiting was excruciating. Brody spent three days pacing back and forth. We kept the VHF radio on, listening for any Coast Guard traffic. I stayed sober and alert. Finally, we got a ping from Holly.

Arrived Grand Cayman. All is well.

They were halfway home and all was well. We were happy to receive the good news. Two days later we got another message.

Leaving Grand Cayman.

We waited again. Brody resumed pacing. We knew we wouldn't hear from them again for several more days, but that didn't ease the tension. It felt like the fate of the world depended on them making it back to Holly's boat. Then they'd really be on a journey. We wouldn't know where they were or how they were doing. This was the last contact we'd have from them in who knows how long. Our lives were on hold until we heard from them again.

Four days passed before we got another message, actually several messages.

Arriving Rio Dulce. All is well.

They had made it!

Daniel staying with me.

We wouldn't be seeing him again anytime soon.

We love you guys.

"We love you too," I said aloud.

"Yes we do," said Brody.

Author's Thoughts

A reader suggested that I read *On Killing: The Psychological Cost of Learning to Kill in War and Society*, by Lt. Colonel Dave Grossman. I suspect she was upset with me for turning Breeze into a killer, and for treating the subject too lightly. I took her advice. When I discovered that it was required reading at the FBI Academy, I decided to use it in the story line, as it tied things together nicely. I probably didn't use it in the way that she hoped, but I appreciate her taking the time to educate me.

I want to thank Jonnie Gee (John Gunter) for his service to our country, and for sharing his experience with me.

The Five Star Veterans Center is a real facility in Jacksonville, Florida. You can donate online at http://5starveteranscenter.org/

Cecil Rogers was an actual smuggler at one time. He wrote a book about his exploits called *Ride the Tide; Adventures of a Pot Smuggler and Tide Rider*. His book can be found at this Amazon link: http://amzn.to/2wdOFl7

*If you enjoyed this book, please leave a review at Amazon.

Acknowledgements

Cover photo by Ed Robinson

Cover Design and Interior Formatting by https://ebooklaunch.com/

Proofreaders: Dave Calhoun, Laura Spink, Jeanene Olson

Final Edit: John Corbin

Other Books in the Series

Trawler Trash: Confessions of a Boat Bum
http://amzn.to/2vzBiyH

Following Breeze
http://amzn.to/2fXJgq2

Free Breeze
http://amzn.to/2fXILfv

Redeeming Breeze
http://amzn.to/2gbBjAx

Bahama Breeze
http://amzn.to/2fJiMe6

Cool Breeze
http://amzn.to/2weKg1l

True Breeze
http://amzn.to/2ws6Hzp

Ominous Breeze
http://amzn.to/2vzLSG5

Other Books by Ed Robinson

Leap of Faith; Quit Your Job and Live on a Boat
http://amzn.to/2fFeJwh

Poop, Booze, and Bikinis
http://amzn.to/2v5G2c9

The Untold Story of Kim
http://amzn.to/2u8yc06

Feel free to contact me with story ideas or if you'd like your name to be used for a character.
Kimandedrobinson@gmail.com

Follow my blog at:
https://quityourjobandliveonaboat.com/

Facebook:
www.facebook.com/quityourjobandliveonaboat/

Made in the USA
Monee, IL
22 September 2020